SECRETS OF A GHOST'S DIARY

Dawn Marie Clifton

For my sons, Kyle, Blake, and Reese
Special Thanks
To my husband and best friend, Stephen, who holds
my heart.
To my beautiful mother, Carolyn, for being my first
reader and believing in me.

CHAPTER ONE

The craziest summer of Carson's twelve years began when he overheard the lighthouse keeper say the ghost was back. Within days, Carson would realize how this phone call would not only change his life, but alter the course of time throughout it.

For the past seven summers, Carson's parents had sent him to stay with his grandparents on St. Simons Island. His grandparents owned and operated the lighthouse, so the news of it being haunted was priority now. Although Carson had never believed in ghosts, the possibility thrilled him. He quickly sent his best friend a 9-1-1 text.

Levi arrived on his skateboard within minutes. The first thing Carson noticed was Levi's hair. It was longer on one side, with black-coffee-colored strands down to his chin. He was two years older than Carson, but the new hairstyle made him look even older. He wore a black T-shirt decorated with a skull, black shorts, and black Vans slip-ons. The odd skater look didn't diminish Carson's excitement, though. He was happy to see his best friend after a long school year apart.

"When did you start skateboarding?" Carson asked, chomping on three pieces of grape bubble gum. He was trying not to stare at Levi's hair, which reminded him of a horse's mane.

"Right after you left last summer," Levi replied. He kicked his board up and caught it.

Carson sat down on the white porch that stretched across the front of his grandparents' red brick house. Levi did likewise.

"You're taller now," Levi said. "But still not taller than I am," he added with a grin. The fun, competitive edge was still alive between the two boys.

Carson *had* grown a couple of inches during the school year, but not much else had changed. He still liked wearing the same kind of button-down shirts with shorts and flip-flops. He smiled, thinking about how good it felt to be back on the island. Bright green grass covered the three acres of land. In the middle of the yard stood a massive angel oak tree, estimated to be five hundred years old. Some of the branches were as thick as the trunks of many trees. The limbs twisted and turned in different directions; it was a tree climber's paradise. In the distance to the left was a small oceanfront cottage. On the right was a sandy beach decorated with palm trees.

Carson glanced toward the towering lighthouse a few yards away before speaking in a confidential whisper. "Early this morning, I overheard the lighthouse keeper on the phone. He said something about the ghost being back."

Levi raised his eyebrows. "No kidding, a ghost? Mike is friends with my mom. He wouldn't make stuff up."

"How does your mom know Mike?" Carson asked.

"My mom acts in plays at the theater. He helps build the sets."

Just then, a gray minivan pulled into the gravel driveway. A girl their age stepped out with a suitcase. Carson thought she resembled a nerd with her tight ponytail and thick glasses. With her mouth puckered as if she'd just tasted a lemon, the slender girl marched up the steps and into the house without saying a word.

"That's my cousin Emma," Carson said as he blew a volleyball-sized bubble.

"Oh, well, she doesn't look too happy to be here," Levi stated as he poked Carson's bubble. It "popped" into a purple mask over Carson's glaring face. "Now you look unhappy, too!" Levi said laughing.

Carson pinched at the sticky mess. "My parents said Emma would be here, but I don't know why. We usually only see her at family reunions. Anyway, this is boring." He paused, then yelled "BOO!" The outburst blew grape breath in Levi's face.

"I don't see how grape gum doesn't get old after all these years," Levi said.

"Why? It isn't the same piece." Carson made a drum roll sound. "Wanna go to the top of the lighthouse?"

"Can we do that later?" Levi asked. "I want to show you the new skate park."

"No. Skate park *later*." Carson stressed the word *later* with a pouty face.

"Still always have to get your way. How about I'll catch *you* later," Levi snapped. He ran off, skateboard in hand. Carson scratched his head, shocked by his friend's reaction. Maybe more than his mane had changed over the year. Today Levi was more like a stubborn donkey than a horse.

Carson perked up at the aroma of frying bacon seeping through the screen door. He raised his head and inhaled with appreciation. Grandma's breakfasts were the best. He skated barefoot across the polished, checkered floor and slid into the arms of a nice grandma hug.

"I get more love when I'm cooking for you!" She did the high-pitched giggle Carson adored.

"I'll hug you again if you've made my favorite biscuits," he said with an arm around her plump shoulders.

"No, the biscuits are all for me," Grandpa said with a smile as he walked into the kitchen. He took a seat at the oval table.

Grandma giggled again. "Carson, go get your cousin. I think she's still upstairs unpacking, dear," she said. "And y'all wash your hands."

Carson rapidly knocked on Emma's door, but she didn't answer. He shrugged and returned to the kitchen, taking a seat next to Grandpa. Emma walked in seconds later and sat down without making eye contact. The cousins sat quietly during breakfast while their grandparents talked about a few needed lighthouse repairs.

After taking his last swig of orange juice, Carson asked the troubling question. "Have you guys heard about the lighthouse being haunted?"

Emma's head shot up with obvious curiosity.

"That's silliness," Grandma stated.

"You two clean the kitchen before you go outside." Grandpa spoke under his napkin while wiping his silver mustache. He winked at his grandkids, and then followed his wife outside. *Way to dodge the question*, Grandpa, Carson thought.

Emma pushed her red plastic glasses higher on her nose. Her eyes appeared cartoonishly big behind the lenses. "Hey, you heard a ghost story?" she asked.

"Oh, you can talk?" Carson responded sarcastically.

"Sorry, I didn't mean to be rude. I'm not exactly happy about being here." Emma sighed as she filled the sink with hot soapy water.

Emma's apology impressed Carson. He didn't ever apologize unless forced to by an adult. While he dried the dishes, he studied his cousin, and realized that they could pass for brother and sister. Both had hair the color of wet sand, and green eyes that Grandma called the emeralds of the sea. The clanking of a pan interrupted his thoughts so he asked, "Why are you so interested in a ghost story?"

"Well, for one, who wouldn't be? And for two, I'm staying in a house *next* to the alleged haunted lighthouse." She made a face that clearly said, "Duh!"

"Point taken," said Carson. "Anyway, I overheard the lighthouse keeper telling someone the ghost is back."

"Who was he speaking with?"

"Don't know; he was on the phone."

She shrugged, "Why not ask him about it?"

"I was eavesdropping when I heard him say it, that's why." It was Carson's turn to make the "duh" face. Emma nodded with understanding.

"You know, my dad is a private investigator, and I've helped him solve cases. I could help you get to the bottom of this if you want." She sounded hopeful.

"Well, my dad is an attorney, so we *might* make a good team." As soon as the words slipped out, Carson realized he had responded without thinking. He and Levi were known as the "summer duet." They would be a trio with Emma in the mix. That was, if Levi still wanted to hang out. If he was going to find out about the ghost, he could definitely use Emma's investigative knowledge. She certainly looked smart, he reasoned with himself.

With the table cleaned and the dishes put away, the two were ready to go outside. Feeling a little more comfortable with her, Carson offered to show Emma around the property, since she hadn't been there for several years.

A gust of wind slammed the screen door against the house when Carson opened it. Salty air from a brewing storm met them on the front lawn, and the blue sky was quickly disappearing behind a curtain of gray clouds. Carson knew from previous summers how powerful storms could develop within minutes at the ocean. His cell phone vibrated, displaying Levi's picture.

Carson answered with a simple, "Hey."

"Hey, I'm headed back to the lighthouse. If there's crazy weather, I want to be where all the action is!"

Levi spent most nights at Carson's place during the summer. Obviously, he was making sure things were cool between them before returning.

"Okay! See you up there," Carson said excitedly.

Levi knew to meet him outside the lantern room at the top of the lighthouse. The most fun always started there.

The lighthouse keeper asked the tourists to leave the lighthouse since severe weather was developing.

Three employees helped maintain the lighthouse during business hours. They stayed during a storm to record activity and communicate with seafaring ships.

The white stone tower faded into the fog. Above, a beacon of light beckoned Carson and Emma. After entering the lighthouse, they stooped low and hid behind the front counter. Grandpa and Mike were studying something on the desk.

"The man with Grandpa…who is that?"

"Yeah, that's Mike, the lighthouse keeper, the one who mentioned the ghost," Carson whispered. He pulled off his flip-flops. "Follow me."

Instead of following, Emma bolted past him. They raced up the cast-iron stairway, spiraling higher and higher. Determined not to be beat, Carson gave it all he had and won by a few steps. He hid the grin of triumph.

Outside on the balcony, the wind was whipping up angrily. Carson thought the ocean looked intimidating, even from the top of the lighthouse, 104 feet up in the air.

The first raindrop thumped Carson on the nose, and then another. Seconds later, he stretched his arm out and couldn't see his hand through the downpour. The balcony door slammed shut. He cupped his hands over his eyes to see if Levi had snuck his way to the balcony yet.

Rain-drenched wind buffeted them. "Carson, we need to go back down!" Emma yelled. She reached for the door and pulled. "The door won't open!"

"That's impossible; it only locks from the inside!" Carson yanked on the handle. It *was* locked. He had assumed the wind blew the door shut, but that didn't explain how it locked. Was Levi playing a trick on him?

A bolt of lightning flashed, highlighting the fear in Emma's eyes. Carson felt scared, too. They were trapped on a metal platform over a hundred feet up, in an electrical storm. Would the wind get strong enough to blow them off? He knew it was possible. The lighthouse balcony Carson loved had suddenly become an edge of death.

⟞⟝

CHAPTER TWO

The balcony door flung open. Relief washed over Carson when he spotted Levi in front of him. Carson quickly pushed Emma through the doorway, then scurried inside behind her, shutting and locking the door in one movement.

"Good grief! Knock me down why don't you!" Levi muttered.

Carson ignored the remark. "Who was in the stairwell?"

"I didn't see anyone," Levi answered with a shrug.

"The door was shut and locked, which can only be done from the inside. You must have passed whoever did it!" Carson paused. "Levi, did you do it?"

Levi raised both hands in the air to prove he had no crossed fingers. "I promise. The door was locked when I got up here."

Carson read honesty in his friend's eyes.

"It must've been the ghost!" Emma said with crossed arms, shivering.

"Wow, I'll never forget the first thing I ever heard you say," Levi said, laughing. "The name's Levi." He nodded with masculine attitude.

She smiled shyly. "I'm Emma."

It was official, Carson thought. Now the "summer trio" could start working on the case.

The spiral stairs seemed ten times longer than usual. Carson didn't want to admit it, but Emma may have been right. What if a ghost had locked them out? Was the ghost trying to kill or scare them? Either way, it was not a friendly gesture. When the ceiling lights suddenly flickered, they jumped down the last set of steps and raced out the front door.

Surprisingly, warm rays of sun greeted them. Farther inland, Carson saw rain clouds, but the threat of bad weather had passed as quickly as it had appeared. A rainbow stretched across a clearing sky.

"The weather is crazy on this island," Emma stated.

"There you guys are," Grandpa said, walking down the porch steps. "Go dry off and change before Grandma catches you. Carson, you know when bad weather hits, you get your behind in the house." Grandpa teasingly swatted him.

After changing clothes, Carson and Levi walked to the new skate park. They took a left out of the driveway and stayed on Lighthouse Road until reaching the old church. After cutting through the connecting cemetery, they crossed a traffic circle. The skate park was on the left about a quarter of a mile, past the barbershop and gas station.

Carson watched Levi do rail stands, kick turns, and moves he couldn't even name. He attempted a few of them, but he couldn't stop thinking about the strange events at the lighthouse. He felt bad for not asking Emma to hang out with them. He tried to justify it by thinking a nerd wouldn't care about skateboarding.

Carson was about to head home when an older boy skated over to Levi. Long bleached-blond hair hung over the right side of his face. *More horsehair,* Carson thought, wondering if skaters ran in herds. Carson felt conflicted about his negative thoughts toward Levi. It wasn't that he was jealous, was he?

"Hey, Levi, want to egg houses with us tonight?" the older boy asked. Levi turned down the invite and quickly skated in the other direction.

Carson wondered if his friend was making bad choices. He knew Levi's mom worked crazy hours, so she wasn't around much, and Levi had never met his dad. Levi was on his own much of the time. "I'm ready to get out of here," Levi whispered.

Carson agreed. They headed toward the road. A few minutes later, the boys walked out of the gas station with their usual drink of choice, a frozen Coke, just the thing for midday summer heat.

"Do you still go to Teddy's barbershop?" Carson asked.

"Not as much, but want to go see him?" They had always liked hanging out with Teddy. True to his nickname, he was a big round teddy bear of a guy, and fun to talk with. He knew all the town gossip and he told the best war stories.

⊨⊰ ⊱⊨

The barbershop was a small, white, stone building with no sign. The faded red and white barber pole had stopped working years ago, but it still marked the business just as effectively. A bell chimed when Carson opened the door. The boys walked into the familiar smell of musk shaving cream.

"*Ee-bow-la-chee!*" Teddy greeted them in a loud Nigerian voice.

Carson walked over and hugged the big, round man.

"Hey, Teddy," Carson said with a smile. The boys jumped up into two empty barber chairs and spun around until their heads swam with dizziness while they listened to Teddy speaking with his customer.

Carson decided to ask the question that was becoming an obsession. "Teddy, have you heard anything about my grandparents' lighthouse being haunted?"

"It's haunted all right." Teddy paused for a moment. Then his gut bounced with laughter. "Come on, boys, you can find other things to get into this summer, can't you?" He diverted the conversation by telling them about the time he had saved his buddy from a grenade. Carson was only half listening. Why didn't Teddy give a direct answer about the ghost? It seemed nobody wanted to talk about it.

Teddy brushed hair off of his customer's neck and removed the long black apron. The man stood and handed Teddy some cash. Tall and skinny as a flagpole, he wore a white Western shirt with silver threading. His shiny belt buckle was large enough to use as a dinner plate.

While Teddy rang him up, the cowboy turned to face the boys. "Ghosts can be dangerous, you two," he spoke in a calm voice. "Teddy is right. Find other things to do this summer." The cowboy smiled and turned around. Placing a black, velvet cowboy hat on his head, he strolled out of the shop.

Carson gazed after him through the dirty window, watching as the man's cowboy boots shuffled across the parking lot toward a vintage red Mustang. When the car was no longer in sight, Carson looked at Teddy for a reaction.

Teddy simply chuckled, saying "Boys, go on home before it gets dark and your Grandma calls me with worry."

As they walked down the road toward home, Carson took a swig of his melted frozen Coke. He crinkled his nose and spit it out. Shaving cream!

Levi bent over with laughter.

Carson popped the lid off the cup, then poured the rest of the drink on Levi's head. They chased each other until their stomachs ached. The boys stopped laughing when they saw Emma on the front porch swing. She looked up from the book she was reading when Carson opened the screen door.

"I think we should sneak into the lighthouse tonight," Emma said with a challenge in her eyes.

Carson pondered the idea with much apprehension. If they did sneak in, it could answer the question haunting him. Still, he wasn't sure if he wanted to know if there was a ghost from personal experience.

"You're not scared are you?" She raised her right eyebrow.

Levi didn't seem to care. "I'm in."

"I'm not afraid," Carson answered, voicing the opposite of what he was feeling.

The low rumble of a car engine at the end of the driveway caught Carson's attention. He turned in time to see an old, red Mustang drive by. Was it the same one from the barbershop? He waited to see if the car turned around, but it didn't.

"Hey," Levi said looking at his cell phone. "Got to go, but I'll be back soon."

Emma scooted off the swing and followed Carson into the house. Carson sat in his favorite blue recliner and started watching an episode of *Shark Week*. Emma sat cross-legged on "the rug of many colors," as Grandpa called it, still reading her book.

After the show was over, Carson asked, "What are you reading?"

"It's a history book of our grandparents' lighthouse," Emma replied.

Carson felt outsmarted. He should have been researching instead of running around all day.

"What did you learn?"

Emma flipped the book to a page she'd marked with a slip of paper and read aloud. "In 1899, after twenty-five years of service, Joseph Martin was found dead at the bottom of the staircase inside the lighthouse. A massive heart attack was determined to be the cause of death. He was forty-five years old at the time, and was remembered as the first lighthouse keeper."

Just then, Levi returned and walked into the den. "Wow, Carson, you look as if you've seen a ghost!"

"Not yet," Emma said laughing. Then she added in a whisper, "Bring a bag on the mission tonight in case we need to..." she paused, "borrow some evidence."

"Your cousin is weird," said Levi. He looked more interested than puzzled though.

"Tell me about it." Carson couldn't believe he had agreed to sneak into the lighthouse. Emma was not the boring geek she resembled.

An hour after their grandparents had gone to bed, the boys and Emma stood at the back door of the lighthouse. Emma had left it unlocked while helping her grandfather close up earlier that evening.

On the ground level of the lighthouse was the museum, a round room with a high ceiling. Historic photos on the walls showed a mix of soldiers and military forts, old building and houses, and random landmarks from around the island. Six glass cabinets housed guns, swords, and various items from the Civil War. A faded confederate flag hung above a soldier uniform.

The smell of the museum always reminded Carson of a dusty leather jacket. Tarnished brass electric lanterns hanging from the walls provided a dim light. A box fan in the far corner produced a low draft.

Carson took charge, since he was the one most familiar with the museum. "Levi, look through the filing cabinet behind the desk. See if you can find the oldest record for lighthouse keepers. Maybe we can learn more about the one that died. Emma, see what you can find in the two chests on the floor over in the corner."

He had no idea what they were looking for, but he had a hunch there were clues in the museum. His dad once told him that a trail of clues stayed behind for anyone who took the time to look.

Emma examined the contents of the first chest with such apparent interest that it prompted Carson to look in the other one. He felt anxious about the possibility that there might be a real ghost. If one did exist, it would present more questions. Carson loved reading mysteries, but now he was living one! *I need an agent name*, Carson thought, *like Maverick.*

He glanced over at Levi thumbing through files. He was the smartest kid Carson knew, although Levi didn't want anyone knowing. He purposely missed questions on school tests so he wouldn't make straight A's. He'd told

Carson once that he didn't want to be labeled a geek, so his intelligence remained a secret.

Emma held up a small scarlet red book with a metal latch on it. "Holy cow, look at this diary! It looks ancient!" She looked happier than a mouse in a cheese house.

Carson reached into the chest before him and pulled out a faded picture, a photo of the staircase inside the lighthouse. Carson recalled Emma reading about the 1899 incident, when a lighthouse keeper was found dead at the base of the stairwell.

Carson gazed at the real staircase. He could see where the body would have fallen. A chill ran down his back. He imagined the man with his mouth gaping open, his wide eyes blank with death. Suddenly, the lights flickered. Carson tried to swallow, but his mouth felt full of cotton balls. He pulled a piece of gum from his pocket, popped it in his mouth, and chewed frantically. The sugary, grape flavor calmed his senses. Chewing gum always improved his focus, but nothing could have prepared him for what happened next.

CHAPTER THREE

Death has come to introduce itself, Carson thought with horror.

"Did you hear that?" Levi whispered. "Someone is in here." He tiptoed across the room and sat on the floor beside Carson. Emma scooted closer to them. She looked as afraid as Carson felt.

Wooden boards creaked as though someone was slowly descending the stairwell. Too frightened to get up and run, the kids huddled with their arms around each other. The flickering lights in the lanterns snuffed out. Cold darkness covered them. The creaking sound grew louder by the second. Then it stopped. The room became deathly quiet.

An overwhelming sensation of being lost and lonely consumed Carson.

Something hit the floor with a loud clatter. An eerie silence followed. The lanterns flickered and blinked back on. Carson turned to look toward where he thought the noise had occurred. Something was on the bottom step.

"What is that?" Levi asked.

"Only one way to find out," Emma replied with a shaking voice.

They cautiously approached the shiny object. Emma's hand trembled as she picked it up.

"It's a beaded necklace." The beads looked like a mixture of gold and pearls. A gold key hung on the end of it.

"I've never seen a key that small," Carson said, examining it.

"Who dropped the necklace there?" Levi asked. "Nobody's in here but us." He looked all around the room. "At least it warmed back up in here."

Nobody spoke the obvious. A look of understanding passed between them. The lighthouse was haunted, just as Mike claimed.

Carson placed the necklace in his bag. "Let's get out of here." Emma and Levi vigorously nodded.

The next morning, Carson woke to the smell of pancakes. His mom often said he could smell food better than a vulture. He stretched his arms up with a yawn, then grabbed a pillow and threw it across the room at Levi's face.

Levi bolted straight up out of sleep and screeched, "I did not kiss her!"

"You didn't kiss who?" Carson asked, laughing. "Let's go eat breakfast, love bird."

Emma was already at the kitchen table when the boys entered the room. She wore a black-and-white polka-dotted shirt. Her hair was pulled back in a tight ponytail again.

Grandpa walked in the kitchen accompanied by a woman with hair like flames of fire and a pointed nose sprinkled with freckles. Her eyes matched the blueberries on the kitchen table.

"Carson, Levi, Emma—this is Ms. Kim. She'll be staying in town for a while."

"Thanks for inviting me for breakfast. Everything smells divine," Kim said in a silky voice.

Grandma set down a tall stack of pancakes. "It's our pleasure to have you here. We're looking forward to seeing your photos of the lighthouse."

"My book is scheduled for publication at the end of the year," said Kim. "This lighthouse will make a beautiful addition to it."

"A book about American lighthouses," Grandpa said, rubbing his chin. "Why didn't I think of that?"

Kim's smile was brilliantly white. "Well, the idea has been done many times before…but *this* book will have a unique twist to it. You just need to wait and see!"

Carson wondered in what way her book would be different, but she obviously wasn't going to disclose that at this time.

"You find a place to stay okay?" grandpa asked.

"Yes, thank you. I don't usually sleep well my first night in a new place," Kim replied.

Something slapped Carson under the table, on the knee. *Did everyone see me jump?* he wondered with embarrassment.

His hand ran across a sticky note. Trying not to look obvious, he read the message: *Meet on the pier with your bag from last night. Ten o'clock. Sneeze if this is agreeable. Emma.*

I'm expected to fake a sneeze? That was ridiculous. He tried to think of how a sneeze sounded and gave it his best shot. The *aaahhh-choo* came out louder than necessary and totally fake-sounding. Emma quietly excused herself. Carson heard her giggling down the hall. It *was* pretty funny.

Emma seemed to be feeling better than she had when she'd first arrived, but he wondered why she had been upset about having to spend the summer there. Who wouldn't want to stay at the lighthouse? After breakfast, he showed Levi the note, and at ten they went to meet Emma.

Carson visited the pier on a regular basis each summer because people-watching could be quite humorous. He was glad to be going there today. As usual, countless colorful umbrellas dotted the beach throughout the many sunbathers. Children were chasing waves sliding to and from the shore. Today, the breeze carried in a mild fishy smell. Out to sea, Carson could see the outline of a shrimp boat. The familiar smells and scene gave him a warm cozy feeling.

Carson noticed Levi's big smile as they approached Emma at the end of the pier. Apparently he wasn't the only one feeling cozy.

Levi said, "Wow, you look like a...normal girl!"

Emma's hair was flowing loose over her shoulders. She wore a yellow tank top with jean shorts.

"Don't be stupid. Did you guys bring the bags?" she asked, blushing.

They sat on the pier and emptied their bags. Emma had the scarlet red book, Carson had the beaded necklace, and Levi had...candy.

"Seriously? Didn't you find any pertinent employee files?" Emma asked with annoyance.

"What do you want to know?" Levi asked, ripping open a bag of Skittles.

"It's all up here in his computer," Carson said, as he knocked on Levi's head with his fist.

"You've got to be kidding me. What was the oldest employee file stored in the personnel cabinet?" she asked sarcastically.

Levi looked up to the sky, rambling off, "John T. Cutter; lighthouse keeper from 1980 to 1993."

"He remembers everything he reads," Carson said. "Practically a photographic memory."

Emma pushed her glasses up and stared at Levi. Carson could practically read the word *wow* on her forehead.

"The historic files must be stored somewhere else in the lighthouse. The cabinet I looked through was only current stuff," Levi said with a mouthful of Skittles. "Want some?" Levi pointed out the pile of candy.

Emma poured some candy into her mouth as Carson explained that Levi kept his intelligence a secret. Emma's eyes lit up when the boys raised their pinkies. They did a three-way pinky swear.

Emma placed the small, scarlet red book in the middle of them. Carson ran his hand over the cover. It felt soft and looked fragile.

"That's a shame. Looks like we might need to break it open since it's locked," Levi said.

"You don't think..." Carson picked up the gold and pearl necklace. He placed the dainty key into the lock. It was a hand and glove fit. When he turned the key, the lock popped open with a click.

"The ghost must have seen me find the book, and then left the key for us," Emma said, looking at Carson.

Carson nodded. "That's right. The ghost showed up and left the key *after* you put the book into your bag."

Levi looked from Emma to Carson. "Wait a minute. Are you two suggesting the ghost *knew* Emma would find the book?"

"Perhaps the ghost *hoped* one of us would find the book. After Emma put the book in her bag, the ghost placed the key on the step so we could open it," Carson paused. "So here goes..."

The moment was interrupted by the sound of swift footsteps walking down the pier. It was Kim, the redhead from breakfast, with a fancy camera hanging around her neck.

"Quick, put the book back in the bag!" Emma whispered.

Carson shoved the contents into his bag. They grabbed some candy and pretended not to see her approaching.

"Oh, what a perfect shot," Kim said, raising her camera and pointing it into the distance. "Oh, hey, kids." She turned and spoke in a sickening, overly sweet voice. She needed acting lessons.

Her fake disposition irritated Carson and he dreaded where this conversation might be headed.

"What's in your bags?" she asked.

Bingo, my intuition was correct, Carson thought.

"Candy, of course," Levi spoke calmly, pointing to the candy pile on the pier. The other two shook their heads in agreement.

"Your name is Carson, right?" She pointed with a long, ivory finger. "What do *you* have in *your* bag?" She tapped her foot.

Levi spoke again. "This is our stuff. Why do *you* want to know?"

"I wasn't talking to you," she snapped at Levi. Then she whispered, "Listen, I'm quite sure I saw you holding something that doesn't belong to you. If I'm wrong, then there's no problem."

Emma had apparently gone into her shy shell, studying her nails.

Carson's mind raced with a million thoughts. *What should I do? If I give her the bag, will she give it back? What does this crazy redhead want? Why is she even here?* He felt his face getting hot. *Who did she think she was? This isn't any of her business. She is not the boss of me!* His emerald eyes blazed with anger.

Carson knew Levi was prepared for what came next, but Emma would have no way of knowing. Her mouth dropped wide open after Carson's next words.

CHAPTER FOUR

"What's the saying? Take a picture, it will last longer!" Carson yelled and held up the bag, dangling it next to his face. He stuck his tongue out as far as it would stretch.

"Run!" Levi yelled.

They sounded like racehorses galloping down the pier. Then, kicking up sand, they sprinted across the beach and stopped at the angel oak. The trunk was wide enough for the three of them to hide behind.

Carson took a peek. "It's all good. She's still on the pier." Levi blew his face up to resemble a blowfish and burst out laughing. Carson joined in, dangling the bag as he had before.

"Have you two lost your minds?" Emma whispered between gritted teeth. She yanked a rubber band off of her wrist, and pulled her hair into a tight ponytail. "I bet Kim is going to tell on us."

"Tell on us for what?" Levi reasoned, "She has nothing on us."

Grandma's voice hollering from the porch interrupted the heated discussion. "Emma, your mother is on the phone for you, dear."

Emma rolled her eyes, turned and walked toward the house with slumped shoulders.

"A call from her mom must not be a good thing," Carson commented.

Levi rolled his eyes. "You're the only one I know with a perfect family, Carson. Anyway, I'm off to the skate park, so...catch you later."

"What about the book?" Carson called after him, feeling abandoned.

"*Later*. We can't look at it without Emma, right?"

Was Levi being thoughtful with the idea of waiting for Emma? No, Carson thought. He doubted Emma would be on the phone long. He felt sure that Levi was using it as an excuse to go skateboarding. Carson was frustrated by the changes he saw in his friend. Would this summer mark the end to their friendship? The question made him feel both sad and frustrated.

Carson looked around the trunk of the tree again. Kim was no longer on the pier, so he ran into the house, into his bedroom, and locked the door. He was playing games on his iPad when three soft knocks interrupted him.

"Who is it?"

There was a moment of silence and then, "Me, Emma."

Carson was surprised it was Emma. He was also surprised to realize he thought of her as a friend already. Emma's dad and Carson's mom were brother and sister. Family was confusing to Carson but he knew that's what made the two of them cousins.

He had never been close to anyone in his family except his parents. He was five years old when his baby sister had died at birth, a fact Carson had never shared with anyone, not even Levi. Carson thought back to Levi's earlier comment about him having a perfect family. Swallowing back complicated emotions, Carson opened his bedroom door. He put on his best pleasant expression. Emma was standing up against the wall as if she shouldn't be there. Carson casually tossed his iPad on his bed. "Hey," he said walking into the hallway.

"I–uh. I'm off the phone now," she stammered.

"Cool. Levi went to the skate park, so maybe we should wait to examine the book."

"Sure, okay." Emma glanced down both sides of the hall, as though she was about to cross a busy street. Carson realized she was feeling awkward. Was she afraid he wouldn't want to hang out with her if the investigation was on hold?

"Wanna go to the gas station with me? I'm out of bubble gum." Carson pulled his jeans' pockets out while making a silly face.

Emma nodded and laughed. Carson could see the tension melt away from her face. They went outside and started walking toward the gas station. He considered asking Emma about the phone call with her mom but he didn't want to risk things getting weird again.

Emma broke the silence. "I was wondering something."

"What?"

"The ghost story case started when you overheard the lighthouse keeper talking on the phone, right?" she asked.

"That's right, when Mike mentioned it."

"Well, I was thinking about where my dad would take the investigation at this point," she said. "What do you think about asking Mike a few questions?"

"Maybe we should, but I can't tell him I was hiding, listening to his conversation."

Emma talked in a teasing tone. "Oh, come on," she kidded him. "We'll just tell him that after you heard his phone call, we broke into the lighthouse. Then when the ghost dropped the necklace, you stole it!"

Carson laughed saying, "I think your ponytail is too tight, and it's affecting the blood flow to your brain."

They were laughing when the low rumble of a car came up behind them.

Carson recognized the engine sound immediately. As the Mustang slowly drove passed, Carson saw the cowboy in the driver's seat.

Emma must have seen Carson staring at the Mustang. "Cool car, huh?"

"Yeah, sure, but the man driving is strange."

"Oh, you know him? I guess this island is small enough to know everyone." Emma stuck her hands in her pockets as they walked along.

"No, I never saw him until Levi and I visited Teddy's barbershop yesterday. Anyway, this cowboy told us that he had experience with ghosts. I don't have a good feeling about him for some reason. He kinda creeped me out." Carson blocked the sun out of his eyes with his hand. "Look, he pulled into the gas station parking lot. Come on!"

"What are we going to do?" Emma asked as they ran side by side.

"We need to sneak into the gas station without him seeing us."

"I don't understand. Why?"

"I don't know, exactly."

They resumed walking once the cowboy had parked and opened his car door. There was still enough distance between them that he wouldn't notice them approaching. Just before he went inside, the cowboy patted his back pockets and suddenly turned around. Carson and Emma stopped dead in their tracks. They watched as he looked down at his key ring and began walking back toward his car.

"He must be going back to get his wallet," Emma said.

"Perfect, let's get inside before he does."

They ran full speed ahead to the double glass doors of the gas station. Carson hoped Ms. Doris, the cashier, would be too busy to notice the door buzzer. He hoped she heard it so much, she didn't hear it anymore, like when his family had lived near a train track. At first, he heard every train, but at some point he got use to the noise and didn't notice it anymore.

Carson quickly swung open the door, allowing Emma to enter first. Then he took her arm and guided her to the corner of the store, where they hid behind a display of Pepsi cases.

"A mountain of drinks, and I am desperately thirsty. This is torture," Emma whispered, staring at the picture of ice sliding down a can of Coke.

Carson responded in his Agent Maverick voice. "*Shush.* Thankfully, Ms. Doris is ringing up a customer or she might have…" Carson stopped speaking when he heard the door buzzer. He held his breath when he heard cowboy boots clunk against the cement floor. Each step grew louder. Carson felt frozen in place. He saw the tip of the snakeskin boots just as Emma pulled him to the left side of the display. He followed her to the candy aisle, and they squatted low to the floor. There was the sound of a refrigerator door opening, then closing. Carson elbowed Emma's shoulder and pointed toward the stacked cases of Coke, and they waddled like ducks back down the candy aisle to their original hiding place. Carson heard the low soothing voice of the cowboy, but couldn't make out the words.

"He must be at the register," Carson whispered. He began tiptoeing toward the front of the store. Emma followed. They stopped behind the frozen Coke machines, straining to hear the cowboy's conversation with Ms. Doris.

"So, are you enjoying the cottage Mr. Jones?" Ms. Doris sounded like the wicked witch from the *Wizard of Oz*, even when she was being nice.

Carson thought it was silly for an adult to call people by their last names, but Ms. Doris seemed to think it made her customers feel valued. Whatever the quirky reason, Carson appreciated her habit since knowing the cowboy's name could be important.

"You can call me Dean," He said politely, "Couldn't ask for a better place to call home," the cowboy replied in the calm voice Carson remembered.

"It certainly has one of the prettiest views on the island," Ms. Doris said. "Will that be all for you?" The cash register drawer dinged open.

"I wasn't going to, but since you asked, I'll take my brand of cigarettes."

Just then the front door buzzer sounded. Carson looked through the small space between the two machines and saw a toddler and her mom walk in. As if pulled by a magnetic force, the toddler walked toward the frozen Coke machines and then around to the back of them. She raised her pudgy little arm, made a small fist, and pointed at Carson and Emma.

"You yike cold dink, too?" the toddler's voice boomed. She had lungs bigger than an elephant.

Her question was followed by dead silence for what seemed like an eternity.

Carson and Emma stared wide-eyed at each other.

"Who's your little cutie talking to?" Ms. Doris asked the mom.

How were they going to explain this? Carson wondered.

CHAPTER FIVE

"Saved by the buzzer" became the famous phrase for the summer trio. Levi walked through the glass doors just in time to see Carson and Emma squirm out from behind the frozen Coke machines. They looked guilty as sin. Levi must have correctly assumed they were hiding from the cowboy at the register.

"Hey! You know the rules. No hiding in businesses," Levi said with his hands on his hips. He intently looked into Carson's eyes.

Carson shot a *play along* look at Emma.

"Sorry, we forgot."

Emma put one hand over the other forming a T and said, "It's my fault. I called time out to get a drink."

Ms. Doris almost turned pea green as she spit out each word, "I've had it with you kids playing in my gas station. Now, buy what you want and get out." She swatted at the air.

The cowboy smiled at Carson. "You have taken my advice and found other things to do, I see," he said with a soft chuckle. As the cowboy strolled out of the gas station, he tilted his hat toward the kids and winked.

Still feeling tense, Carson felt compelled to buy not one, but three packs of grape bubble gum. He also bought himself, Emma, and Levi a frozen Coke for the hot walk home. Even an alligator would complain about this much humidity.

"Thanks for saving us, Levi. Pretending to play hide-and-seek was brilliant," Emma said with a smile. She pushed her glasses up and looked to be waiting for a response.

Levi shrugged without saying a word. Carson figured he didn't know how to respond to a compliment.

Carson broke the silence. "We were hiding from the cowboy. We learned that his name is Dean Jones and he lives in a waterfront cottage."

Emma shrugged. "He must be seven feet tall, but he seems nice."

"You probably thought he was cute," Levi said, gently yanking on her ponytail.

"Gross!" Emma gently pushed Levi. She suddenly stopped walking. "This place creeps me out. Can we go a different way?" She frowned at the cemetery in front of them.

"Not unless you want to walk the long way," Carson replied. It was a large cemetery crowded with different-shaped headstones. Most of the slabs looked old, with cracks and black mildew on them. Some had sunk in places and protruded crooked out of the ground. They looked forgotten about, with no flowers or mementoes in sight. Walking through the cemetery reminded Carson of the ghost. "I didn't believe in ghosts until the lighthouse incident last night. I wonder if this one's dangerous."

Levi whispered as if the buried people underneath their feet could hear him. "First of all, I've read that one in five people has seen or felt a ghost, so I *did* believe in them. Secondly, locking the two of you on a lighthouse balcony during a storm qualifies them as dangerous."

"I disagree," Emma whispered back. "I think the ghost was only trying to get our attention."

A small tree branch fell and hit Levi on the head. He rubbed his head. "OUCH!" The gray branch lying on the ground resembled a human bone, Carson thought. So did Emma and Levi, judging by their stunned expressions.

A black cat jumped on top of a headstone in front of them, hissing, its fur sticking up. The kids took off running all the way back to the angel oak. Out of breath, Carson leaned against the rough bark of the massive tree. "Whew. Back where we started."

"It's time to open the book," Emma stated matter-of-factly.

"Levi, stay here and keep watch. Text me if Kim comes around," Carson said.

⊨⊰ ⊱⊨

While Emma snagged three packs of cheese crackers from the kitchen pantry, Carson went to his room to get the mysterious book. It bewildered him to see his bedroom door slightly ajar. He always kept the door shut. Pulling a piece of gum out of his pocket, Carson used his foot to push the door wide open. His iPad was on his bed where he had tossed it. Where was the book? He stuck the grape gum in his mouth. Sugar woke his senses. A cold presence slithered up behind him, and the hairs on the back of his neck stood to attention. He instinctively turned around, but he saw no one. *It must be the ghost.* Was the ghost upset at him for losing the book? The contents would be easily accessible with the key still in the lock. The need to find it, consumed him.

Carson dropped to his stomach, and slid under his bed to search for the book, thinking it might have fallen when he got up to answer Emma's knock. The bed shifted above him, as if someone had sat on the mattress. He heard a muffled noise that sounded like glass shattering. Scooting back out from under the bed, he banged his head against the metal beam, but adrenalin blocked the pain.

He stared in disbelief at his pillow lying on the floor. Carson crawled over and lifted the bulky pillow into the air. With goose bumps from head to toe, he stared at a broken picture on the floor. Next to it was the scarlet red book.

He remembered. Earlier, when he was distracted by wondering if Levi had made an excuse to run off to go skate-boarding, he hid the book under his pillow. It occurred to him that he needed to stay focused on the case. To be distracted was to lose control of the investigation.

Carson slipped the picture out of the broken frame, grabbed the book, threw both in the bag, and darted out of the house.

Back at the massive tree, Emma was tapping her foot, clearly out of patience.

Levi asked with crossed arms, "What took you so long?" He didn't wait for a response. "You're slower than a turtle with a weight problem."

"I had an encounter…" Carson paused. Telling them he had lost the book, even for a minute, wouldn't be cool. "Never mind. Let's find a secluded place before something else happens."

"I know the perfect place, just around the corner," Levi said.

Emma jumped up and down with her hands over her mouth, as if she were stifling a scream.

Carson smiled from ear to ear and shared her apparent excitement about opening the book at last.

From the angel oak, Levi took them in a straight line to the beach. They turned left, following the shoreline for about half a mile.

Carson would never have seen the old shack, fifty yards inland and hidden by overgrown shrubs and crooked trees. It was a perfect hideout. Based on the white stuff splattered all over it, local pelicans and their friends used it as a resting place. Perhaps it was bombing practice, Carson thought with a smirk.

It took a few minutes for Carson's eyes to adjust to the darkness after the trio entered the shack. Did someone live there at one time? He couldn't imagine living in such a small space. There were no bedrooms, living room, or kitchen. It was a simple square room with one window. Under the window was a wooden table for two, but the chairs were missing.

Carson used his shoulder to wipe a running bead of sweat from his brow as he took a sniff. The shack's smell reminded him of when his dad burned leaves in the fall. "Seems like someone has used the woodstove recently," Carson said, pointing to the corner. The black iron rectangular box sat on four short legs. The front of it was open with a round door, and a long handle. A pipe went from the back of it and up through the ceiling.

"There's no way anyone but me has been here lately. This is my secret hideout," Levi responded, a bit defensively.

"Come on guys, put the book on this table," Emma suggested.

The book felt soft and fragile in Carson's hand. Since he had unlocked it earlier, Carson pulled the key out and laid it on the table. He pushed the button to release the strap that held the cover closed. Then he slowly opened it to the first page. Carson read aloud.

April 17, 1893—Diary of Minnie Mae Murphy, to always remember....

Dear Diary,

It is to this day exactly three months since my escape off the dreadful pirate ship, Grande Surge. I am excited about this place called St. Simons Island. I can hear the ocean from my bed and it soothes me like an old friend. It seems I belong here, the way everything is working to my good.

Tomorrow, I start a job at the lighthouse. It was rather humorous how Mr. Martin seemed suspiciously yet pleasantly surprised by my knowledge of ships and the ocean.

I already feel a connection with the lighthouse. Without it, I would have perished. It was, indeed, my savior.

Freedom is nothing short of bliss. Alas, I will never take it for granted. I have used a small part of the treasure to establish myself, but plan to repay it.

I have moved the burial site, and have not decided whether to document the location in this diary or not. I feel no guilt in hiding it, for without question, the unique treasure does not belong to pirates. I fear if something happens to me, it will be lost forever.

CHAPTER SIX

Carson, Emma, and Levi were standing bent over with arms crossed on the small table. Rays of sunshine lit up the opened diary in the middle of them.

"Holy cow! I wonder if the treasure is still buried somewhere around here?" Levi asked, with his pupils practically the shape of dollar signs.

Emma ignored the comment. "Look at the dates. The lighthouse keeper she wrote about must be the Joseph Martin we were reading about, the one who died in the lighthouse."

"The year this was written lines up with that assumption, for sure," Carson agreed.

"Hello, did you two dorks not hear the last part about a treasure?" Levi asked.

"Do you think he's the ghost?" asked Carson.

"Minnie Mae worked at the lighthouse," Emma chimed in. "The diary and key necklace belonged to her. I think she's the ghost. Now, we need to figure out *why* she is haunting us."

Levi raised his voice. "*Maybe* she wants us to find the buried treasure?"

"There are so many questions," Carson said, looking at Emma. "Where do we begin? Your investigative skills need to kick in now." He saw her confidence level grow and this made him feel good.

"I think we need to start by reading the entire diary," she suggested.

Levi snagged the diary up from the table. "When I read a book, I start at the end." He turned to the last page. "Figures…look, it's been torn out." Levi held the diary up as if reading to a class. Part of a jaggedly torn page protruded out of the binding.

Emma took the book. "Maybe the page right before it will help us understand why it's missing." She flipped to the previous page.

August 7, 1899

Dear Diary,

I lost my friend. His blood is on my hands, though I am not the one who caused his death. My secrets have caused such stress. It cannot fall in the wrong hands, but the burden of them I should have kept to myself.

I feel lost and alone.

The only thing I know for sure is that drawing a map for the treasure is now appropriate. I have relocated it twice since my arrival, and now, on the day of his funeral, it's in its final resting place.

After I am gone, it is my hope that destiny will suffice, and bring the treasure into the right hands at the right time.

It must not be a coincidence; the last page of this diary will contain the most valuable secret of all.   ~Minnie Mae Murphy

"I knew it," Levi grumbled. "Someone stole the map to a buried treasure."

"The diary has been in this bag," Carson said, pointing to the bag on the table, "or in my room since we found it. Who could have taken it?"

"The map could have been stolen a long time ago," Levi pointed out.

Emma studied the torn page. "This tear is fresh. The ridge where it was torn is brighter than the rest of the page."

"I need a piece of gum," Carson said, pulling a pack of gum out of his back pocket. He thought back to when the ghost haunted them in the lighthouse, and then again when he was alone in his room.

"Lost and alone…" he whispered.

"Is that gum making you senseless?" Emma asked, "What are you talking about?"

"Minnie Mae wrote that she felt lost and alone in her last entry." Carson took the diary and pointed to the words.

"The two times I've encountered her, I've had the same feeling—of being lost and alone."

"What do you mean," Emma began, and Levi finished the question with her, "*two times?*"

"Oh, no," Carson began chewing as if his life depended on it.

"Yep," Levi said smiling at Emma. "All this grape sugar has turned Carson's brain into a glob of chewing gum."

Carson's brow crossed in such concern that Levi felt bad for joking around. He asked, "What's wrong?"

"When I went to get the book from my room, the door was open. I never leave my bedroom door open." He told them about the earlier ghost encounter in his room.

"You thought the ghost was mad because you had forgotten where you put the diary," Emma said, "but she was mad because someone stole the map."

Carson shook his head. "I'm afraid that might be the case." He reached in the bag and took out the picture. "This is what got knocked off the wall." He placed the picture of the lighthouse on the table where the only sliver of sunlight remained.

After they hunched over to get a better look, a dark and cold shadow covered them. The lost and lonely feeling returned, washing over Carson like a strong ocean wave. He grabbed the edge of the table with shaking hands. The sound of chattering teeth echoed in Carson's head.

As if winter had stolen summer, Carson watched the breath from Emma and Levi's lungs drift into the air. Then realized he was holding his. *Breathe,* he thought, *or you're going to pass out.* Pages of the book began turning by an invisible hand, and then stopped. The book stayed open, beckoning them to read the diary entry.

The shadow flew into the woodstove, igniting a blazing fire inside. Carson felt the warmth of it from where he stood at the table. The smell of smoke filled his nose. As he exhaled slowly, he felt himself starting to relax. The fire felt like a gesture of gratitude. Carson realized it was because they had begun investigating the diary.

The summer trio had been chosen to know the secrets of Minnie Mae's diary. The question haunting Carson now was *why?* He had a sick feeling in his stomach as he contemplated the possibilities of danger.

It was logical to think that the person responsible for taking the map would be greedy. Carson knew from reading books that greed drove people to do irrational things. This could be bad. An unspoken voice, like a cozy feeling, lured them to the wooden floor in front of the warm stove. Quietly sitting cross-legged, the three kids listened to the crackling of the burning fire.

Carson still held the picture, and Emma held the diary, opened to the page selected by the ghost.

"Well, making a fire for us was nice of her." Levi looked mesmerized. Leave it to Levi to say something carefree in a tense moment.

Emma held the diary up in the firelight and began reading aloud.

April 1, 1898

Dear Diary,

Today, five years after my escape, I saw Captain Robert Riley. Thankfully, he did not see me. I am confident that by now, the captain knows the treasure is missing.

I asked a lighthouse coworker and friend to listen around the docks for questions that the captain or other pirates might be asking about my whereabouts.

I never told anyone on the ship my real name, and I have changed my appearance since they last saw me. Surely, this will ward off any chances they have of finding me, and thus the treasure, too.

I have been asked by people why I have never married. I have never shared with anyone that Joseph asked for my hand, and that I answered no. I will never marry.

As the captain would say, "It just isn't in the cards for me." This is the only statement of truth he spoke over me. For all else, I make my own destiny.

Emma looked up from the diary, "I think Minnie is trying to draw our attention to either the captain or to Joseph."

Carson held the five-by-seven photograph up to the fire-light. "I don't see anything significant about this picture."

Levi leaned over to take a look at it. "When we get back to your grandparent's house, let's examine it under a magnifying glass."

"I've never seen one around the house."

"But there are plenty of reading glasses around the house," Emma said.

"Way to be observant," Carson nodded with appreciation.

He looked at his cell phone when it vibrated. "It's Grandma," he mouthed silently. "Hello. Yes, ma'am, we are headed back. Love you, too. Bye."

They stood up and dusted off their shorts.

"What about...?" His question went unfinished when suddenly the fire went out on its own. Carson shook his head. "This summer is getting crazier by the minute."

Shortly after, the kids entered a strangely quiet living room. Grandpa usually had the television turned to the News at this time. He was religious about it.

They followed the voices, coming from the kitchen. A police officer sat at the kitchen table with the grandparents, sipping on a cup of coffee. Drinking coffee in the evening? Decaf or not, this couldn't be a good thing.

"Kids, why don't you have a seat?" the officer said, as he set his coffee cup on the table.

Carson glanced at his grandparents for some kind of reassurance, but they simply nodded their agreement with concerned expressions.

Carson wondered if this had something to do with Levi, and the company he kept lately. Was the summer trio being blamed for egging or some other crime?

Carson tried to read Levi's face, but it resembled stone. He looked at Emma, who strangely wore an expression of pure determination. She tightened her ponytail as if contemplating her battle plan. Carson realized he respected his cousin, and feared what his friend Levi must have brought on them.

CHAPTER SEVEN

The kitchen offered a divine smell of Italian marinara. Carson's stomach growled like a lion, and he wondered if meatballs would be part of the cuisine. The aroma made him much more irritated at the presence of this uniformed intruder.

Levi was apparently anxious to get things out in the open as well. "What seems to be the problem, officer?" He sounded like a movie actor, Carson thought.

The three kids sat down at the kitchen table across from the officer. Carson hung his bag on the back of his chair so it would be out of view. Did this have anything to do with the diary? Silently, they waited. Carson began counting down.

The officer removed his hat and placed it on the table in what seemed to be slow motion. His pitch-black hair was perfectly parted on the side and slicked back, with not a strand out of place. The officer stared at each of them, one at time. Was it some kind of cop tactic so they would break down, confessing every sin ever committed? Carson counted down again, this time in rhythm with the ticking of a grandfather clock standing in the left corner. Ten, nine, eight, seven…

Something about the cop seemed familiar to Carson, but he knew that couldn't be possible. Thank goodness, he never had encounters with police before. Four, three, two…

"Sir, how can we help you?" Emma asked, breaking the uncomfortable silence.

The officer's black mustache twitched, reminding Carson of sniffing bunny whiskers. When Levi made a snorting noise, the mustache twitched double time. *This cop was so serious, it was hilarious.* Carson covered his grin with his hand.

Grandpa put a stop to the humor. "You three listen up, now. Have some respect for the law."

Carson had never heard his Grandpa be so stern. He felt bad that his grandparents had been put in an awkward situation. They sat their hands in their laps, looking down at them.

The officer cleared his throat and said, "I'm afraid I have some bad news."

The trio's heads shot up at the same time.

"Teddy's barbershop was burned to the ground today. The fire was out of control by the time the fire trucks arrived. There is nothing left of it."

Levi and Carson turned to look at each other.

"*Who's* barbershop?" asked Emma with eyebrows scrunched together.

"Our friend Teddy," Carson somberly replied. He looked back at the officer. "Is Teddy okay?"

The officer interrupted. "I need to ask the three of you some questions."

"Sir, I'm sorry, but you need to answer my question first," Carson demanded. "Is Teddy all right?" Carson was sure his first chest hair sprouted.

"Teddy is being treated for smoke inhalation at the hospital. We think he will be fine."

Carson heard Levi's exhale of relief as he asked, "What does this have to do with us?"

The question was ignored. Officer Browne pulled out a small pad and pen from his shirt pocket and wrote something down. The guy took the trophy for most annoying person ever. The cop's gold badge was in the shape of a shield with an eagle perched on top. Above it, the name Stanley Browne was stitched into the dark blue shirt.

Levi sounded irritated this time. "Sir, if you are accusing us of something, I have to tell you—we were on the beach today, and nowhere near Teddy's shop."

Officer Browne wrinkled his nose as if he smelled a clue. He proceeded to write again.

Carson noticed the gold ring on the cop's finger. It was triangle shaped, with a red stone fitted in the center. *Cool ring for a big dork.* It looked out of place.

"Can anyone verify your location on the beach?" he asked.

"Sure…well…" Levi's voice drifted off.

Carson could envision the cop's whiskers flying off his face if they told him the truth. To say their only witness was a ghost.

"We were at the gas station earlier today. We bought gum and Cokes," Emma chimed in. "What time was the fire?"

Oh no, Carson thought.

"Oh, so you *were* near the barbershop then?" He began scribbling ninety miles an hour with his pen. There wasn't that much stuff to be writing. Carson rolled his eyes and bit his lower lip. He could feel some choice words begin to crawl up his throat. This wasn't a good time to lose his temper, but between the smell of yummy marinara sauce and this strange officer, he was getting close.

With clenched teeth Carson repeated Emma's question, "What time was the fire, *sir*?"

Officer Browne acted as though he didn't hear the question. He stood up abruptly, shook Grandpa's hand, and said, "That will be all for now. Thanks for your time, folks."

He snatched his hat off the table as if someone was racing him to it. Then he carefully placed it on his head using both hands. Strutting out of the kitchen, he turned and added, "Don't be talking to Teddy about this visit, or the fire. It would be best if you stayed away from that part of town."

Why? Carson wanted to ask, but didn't.

Everyone ate spaghetti and meatballs in silence. Carson couldn't enjoy it after the bothersome visitor. Plus he was worried about Teddy. *How did the fire start? Was someone trying to hurt Teddy? What if this had something to do with the diary or buried treasure? Why did Officer Browne tell them to stay away?*

⊷⊱ ⊰⊶

After dinner, Grandpa asked Levi to go home for the night. "You know we care about you, Levi, but we need to have a family meeting. Carson will let you know when it's a good time to come back."

Carson winced at the pain in Levi's face. Levi silently slid his chair under the table. He staggered out the back door with slumped shoulders. Carson glanced at Emma in time to see a tear run down her cheek.

"You two look exhausted. This meeting can wait until morning," Grandpa said. Hugs were given before going to their room.

While they cleaned the kitchen, Carson told Emma about Teddy. He described Teddy's fun-loving personality and all the meaningful time they had spent with him in the barbershop over the years.

"Teddy sounds like a wonderful man, Carson. I'm sorry he was hurt." There was sympathy in Emma's eyes.

She lowered her head when saying, "I feel bad the way Grandpa made Levi go home. Do you think we'll be able to see him again?"

"I'm sure we'll be able to clear things up. After all, we haven't done anything wrong."

"What about breaking into the lighthouse and taking the diary?" she asked.

"Nobody knows. Plus, it has nothing to do with the fire."

"Kim knows something about the diary I think. What if this was her way of getting back at us for standing up to her at the pier?"

"That doesn't make any sense, Emma," Carson sounded grumpier than he intended.

"Well, neither does your hang-up with the cowboy, now, does it?" she snapped back.

"Look, I'm sorry. I'm just tired, so I'll see you in the morning," Carson said yawning. It was the first time he had apologized to someone on his own and he meant it.

Carson thought back to Emma's arrival. Soon, he would feel comfortable enough to ask why she had been upset when she arrived and also when her mom called. He felt cheated now that he knew how much fun a cousin could be. Why did his family have to live so far apart? He was from Florida. Emma lived with her parents and older sister in Nevada. Family reunions were here on St. Simons Island in Georgia but happened rarely.

Carson threw his pillow and blanket back onto his bed. Something fell with a thump onto his big toe. A word he was not allowed to say shot through his mind. He glared at the silver object on the floor—a cigarette lighter. What was it doing in his room? He picked it up, and flipped the lid with his thumb. Then he rolled the small metal wheel. When the flicker ignited, he slammed the lid and threw the lighter across the room.

Carson's thoughts developed into a tornado of images from the day. He covered his eyes when the ghost's fire in the stove flashed before his eyes. He covered his ears when the officer's voice echoed in his head, "Teddy's shop burned, burned, burned…"

Carson dropped to his knees and crawled over to the lighter, which had landed in his Spiderman beanbag chair. Still on all fours, without touching it, he examined the side facing up. He picked up the silver metal object with a sock. Something resembling three fancy "M" s had been engraved on it.

The lighter had been used a lot by its owner, judging by the worn corners. This caused Carson to think it had been accidently dropped rather than planted. Then again, maybe this had been used by the person responsible for the fire at Teddy's shop. If so, his fingerprints were on the possible tool used to start the fire. He frantically wiped the surface with the sock. What if the arsonist left this in his room as a threat?

It was late, but Carson wanted to hear the sound of his mom's voice. His phone had the capability to "video-chat." He did this weekly with his parents during summer.

Carson picked up his phone just as a text message displayed. It was from Levi. It read, "The cop was a fake."

CHAPTER EIGHT

Carson was thrilled to have one of the best aromas in the world welcome him to the new day. The scent of cinnamon rolls awakened his belly and saliva glands.

Grandpa sat at the kitchen table with the morning paper in hand when Carson strolled through the entryway. Grandpa gave him a wink. Grandma stood at the stove, scrambling eggs. Carson put his arm around her, giving the usual, "Thank you for making food" hug. Her giggle filled his left ear. The situation wasn't as dreadful as it seemed last night.

Emma was frowning when she took her seat at the table. Carson noticed she didn't have her glasses on, and figured it was so her bloodshot eyes wouldn't be magnified. Grandpa reached over and planted a kiss on Emma's cheek.

Carson was glad Grandpa waited to discuss Officer Browne's visit until after he gobbled down a third cinnamon roll. He was licking the frosting off his thumb when the meeting came to session. One second all seemed well, the next it plummeted. This is what mom meant when she called life an emotional rollercoaster, Carson thought.

Grandma stood behind Grandpa's chair, her hands on his shoulders. It appeared they were a unified team. Grandpa's voice was gentle, yet firm. "We've decided not to tell your parents about Officer Browne's visit, unless something else happens. Carson, I am sure you've seen a change in Levi. We've heard he is in unruly company lately. We are not saying he had something to do with the fire, but we want to guide you toward a decision not to associate with Levi until things get cleared up. Is this understood?"

"Yes, sir," Carson responded but was thinking, *No way, José.*

Emma nodded.

"You two, go have fun. I'll clean the kitchen," Grandma patted both their heads.

Carson and Emma sat on the back porch steps. The morning air was already warm and sticky. An orange biplane emblazoned with red and yellow flames cut through a blue sky above the beach. Orange smoke gusted out behind it, making figure eights between patches of clouds. Carson could almost feel the G-forces during its vertical descent toward the ocean. The engine sounded like a deflating balloon as it propelled back up, twirling around and around.

Carson turned to see Emma staring down at the grass. Surely even a bookworm would find a free airshow exhilarating. Then it hit him; she probably couldn't see it without her thick glasses.

"Do you need to get your glasses?"

She jerked her head up, as if startled. "No, I'm wearing contacts."

"Oh, so why do you normally wear glasses?"

"So people don't call me baby names. I hate being called stuff like, *cutie* or *sugar.*" She shrugged, adding, "I'm taken seriously when I wear glasses."

Carson nodded with understanding.

He was thinking about asking why she had been crying when she announced it. "My parents are probably getting a divorce. They sent me here so they could decide for sure."

Carson knew what divorce was from some of his friends back home. "That sucks," he lamely said, wanting to say more but not sure how to make her feel better.

It seemed stating the fact had made Emma feel a little better. She changed the subject, "So what are we going to do about Levi?"

"The way I heard it, Grandpa said he wanted to *guide* us. Being guided makes it optional, right?"

Emma slightly smiled. "I totally agree."

Carson raised his face toward the sun, basking in its warmth, as the biplane did another flyby. The flames on the side caused Carson to replay what happened in the shack with the ghost yesterday. He thought of the barbershop fire conversation with the fake cop. Carson told Emma about the lighter he found in his room and the text he had received from Levi.

"The officer seemed legit to me," Emma responded, "How would Levi know he was a fake?"

They sprang to a standing position and whirled around when Kim's voice suddenly piped in, "Aren't there more interesting things to do around her than sit on a porch? You're on an island!"

⇥ ⇤

How long had she been listening? The overriding goal was to get out of her presence ASAP. What a nosy nincompoop. Carson didn't hide his look of annoyance. He blurted, "We're headed to the lighthouse right now, actually. We're helping Mr. Mike today."

Kim attempted an innocent-sounding cackle. "I doubt that."

She held something out, causing Carson to almost swallow his tongue. It was his bag. He had left it on the back of his chair last night, forgetting to take it to his room after the "cop" left. Distracted yet again.

He patted his pockets in need of gum, but all he had was the lighter. His nerves buzzed around like bees in a hive. Emma glared at him. This would be the second time he lost track of the diary; her eyes practically spit the words.

Carson thought Kim nearly sang opera, trying to sound genuine. "Listen, kiddies, we had a misunderstanding on the pier. Can you consider this a peace treaty? I'd like us to start over." Her long ivory arm held out the bag.

Carson leaped up four steps in one stride and snatched the bag out of her grasp. He reached inside. Everything was there.

"Thanks." What else could he say?

"Don't mention it. See you dolls around. Ta-ta!" Kim said, as she pranced, deer-like, down the porch steps.

Emma grabbed the bag from Carson, slinging it over her shoulder. "You are no longer in charge of this," she stated.

"Agreed." Yet again, what else could he say? Girls were getting the best of him today.

"We need to go somewhere and make sure everything is in here."

Carson looked up at the lighthouse balcony. "Nobody is up there, so come on." He automatically reached for his phone to text Levi, but then remembered. Emma gave him a knowing look. "Next time," she reassured him. For now, it was a summer duet after all.

There were a couple of customers leaving the museum when Carson and Emma went inside. Mike was lighting up several vanilla-scented candles placed high and low throughout the museum. Carson knew he did this simple daily chore for two reasons: one, Grandma didn't care for the dusty museum smell, and two, Grandma said she liked the historic atmosphere candles created.

Mike glanced up and said, "Carson, I haven't met your cousin yet."

Carson felt awkward doing introductions, but he used his best manners. "Emma, this is Mr. Mike, the lighthouse keeper."

Emma was comfortable enough to shake his hand. "It's nice to meet you, sir. How long have you been the lighthouse keeper?"

He set the matches down. "Well, I've been working here with your grandparents for two years now."

"You must have a lot of interesting stories you could tell us," Emma said.

Carson knew Emma was in investigator mode, but he wasn't sure it was time to fish for information after last night's drama.

Mike gazed up in thought. "Let's see, now, I would say it depends on what you think is interesting. I bet Carson here would tell you that every lighthouse has its secrets," he said with a chuckle.

Carson spoke faster than his tongue could move. "No, I don't know any secrets."

Mike didn't seem to notice Carson's discomfort. He started stroking a match, which refused to light as he said, "A lighthouse is the perfect conductor of light, and its beacon will never lead you into darkness."

This obviously impressed Emma. "Wow, spoken as beautifully as Shakespeare."

Mike continued to struggle with the match. "This silly task will take me all day, at this rate." He shook his head.

Carson counted five more candles to light. He felt compelled to help, so he took the lighter out of his pocket and lit the others.

Mike stared at Carson. "Hey, thanks, Carson. Now I can get on to the real duties of a lighthouse keeper." He took a seat at the desk and gave them a polite nod.

Carson didn't hang around for another second. He bolted up the stairs. One hundred twenty-nine steps later, they were on the balcony.

Emma asked, "Are you sure we should close this door?"

"Sure," Carson paused. "I'll put my flip-flop in the doorframe."

"Can I take a look at the lighter?" Emma asked.

He handed it over. They sat on the balcony with their backs leaned against the lamp room. The breeze coming off the ocean cooled Carson's warm face.

A big pink-and-orange-beaked pelican with black-tipped wings flew next to the lighthouse. The bird bent his head toward them, as if greeting his own kind. Carson figured since they were up so high, it was understandable.

"Don't you think every pelican needs a black top hat to wear?" Carson asked jokingly.

"I think you need your head checked." Emma bonked his head with her fist. "You, a twelve-year-old kid, pulls a cigarette lighter out of his pocket in front of an adult."

Carson put his hands on his head in frustration. "I don't know why I keep messing up. My mind is fuzzy with so much craziness happening."

Emma pulled the rubber band off her wrist, and pulled her hair back into a ponytail.

"We need to organize all the events and the questions we have on paper. Then come up with a to do list."

"Sounds like a plan."

"Oh, by the way, I have one mystery solved," she said.

"What?"

"The cigarette lighter was not planted in your room. It was dropped by accident," she said, standing.

"How do you know?"

"Everyone knows fingerprints can be wiped off. If the purpose of leaving the lighter was to make you look guilty, the culprit would have placed it where it would implicate you—maybe in your dirty laundry or your bathroom sink. Also, this cigarette lighter wasn't some random, cheap, over-the-counter item. The condition of the lighter indicates that the person has owned it for years. It's engraved. My guess is this marking is significant to the owner. It's obviously used a lot. The intruder lost this lighter by accident. And, most likely, the person who dropped it is the same person who went in your room and stole the treasure map from the diary."

Carson thought about what his cousin said for a moment. He shook his head with a smile. "You need to wear those glasses of yours," Carson said laughing, "because they fit your genius personality very well."

CHAPTER NINE

Emma and Carson examined the diary to make sure Kim hadn't taken any pages. "We're lucky. No ripped-out pages. Plus the key and picture haven't been tampered with," said Emma.

"I still don't like her," Carson said flatly.

"Do you like any adults?" Emma said with a chuckle.

"I like Teddy, and Ms. Doris at the gas station is okay sometimes, even though she sounds like the wicked witch of the west." Carson did a witch's laughing impression as Emma covered her ears.

His act was cut short when Mike interrupted. "Hey, we have some customers on the way up, so let's take this ear-piercing noise elsewhere," he said.

They could hear Mike descending the staircase.

"See, that's one reason I don't trust some adults," Carson whispered. "They keep sneaking up on us." Emma rolled her eyes.

After they reached the bottom of the spiral stairs, Mike watched them head toward the exit. "Carson!" Mike called out, just when he was about to open the door.

They turned around. Carson said, "Yes, sir?"

"That lighter came in handy earlier. Sure would make my job easier if I had one. What do you say?"

"Well, you see, it's not mine. It's my...Grandpa's," he lied.

Mike walked over with an outstretched hand. "Oh, perfect then. I'll just use it here in the lighthouse, and then he'll never know you had it."

Was Mike threatening to tell if Carson didn't hand it over? Carson wondered why the luck Emma had mentioned had suddenly disappeared. He reluctantly took the lighter out of his pocket and placed it in Mike's open left hand. With a smile, Mike flicked the top up with his thumb and ignited it. After he shut the lid, he gave it a small toss up in the air and caught it. "Thanks Carson. I really appreciate it." He sounded sincere.

Carson hadn't noticed the gold ring on Mike's hand before.

"Congratulations, sir. When did you get married?" Carson nodded toward Mike's left hand. Mike shook his head as he walked behind his desk.

"Married? No not me. Marriage skips every other generation in my family," he said, chuckling. "It's a wonder the family name hasn't gone extinct."

Customers were trying to come through the museum door, so Emma and Carson left. They walked over to the angel oak, and leaned up against the trunk. Carson was still wishing he had some gum. At lunchtime, grabbing a pack would be imperative.

⚔ ⚔

"What got into you?" Emma asked with crossed brows. "Was that nervous chatter? I've never seen you say more than three words to an adult unless you had to."

"What is this? Are you interrogating me now?" Carson returned the questions with crossed arms.

"Don't take your frustration out on me," she replied. "Besides, it was fine to give Mike the lighter. We already learned what we needed to from it."

"All right, I feel better then." Carson slid down to the ground with his back against the trunk. He was about to point to a shrimp boat out to sea when something white, wet, and smelly plastered the bridge of his nose. He looked up since it was the only direction it could have come from. A choir of gray and white sea gulls filled the upper branches of the Angel Oak. The noise they made sounded like a crowd at a basketball game after someone scores. They were apparently pleased with the points one of the birds had earned.

Emma hit the ground with her knees, laughing hysterically. "I'm sorry, Carson. I just can't believe your luck today," she said between breaths. "Let's go in so you can clean up the mess, or before I get hit."

Silently, Carson stood up and followed a giggling Emma to the house. Maybe later, he would think this was funny, but he doubted it. Luckily, his lunch appetite hadn't been ruined, since their grandparents took them to the best burger and ice cream joint on the island.

Carson, Emma, and their grandparents sat outside at a picnic table that had an umbrella in the center. The beach music playing made many of the walking tourists smile. An older couple in the vacationing spirit began dancing on the sidewalk. Grandma said Southerners' called it "shagging."

Carson was experiencing a cold ache in his front teeth while biting into his double-fudge ice cream cone when Levi appeared. Levi stood in front of their table, a police officer at his side.

Carson noticed Emma's face light up despite the fact that Levi was with a cop. The officer spoke first. "I'm sorry to bother y'all, but I was planning on coming by the lighthouse to speak with you. Since we all happen to be here, do you mind if I take a minute of your time?" he asked the grandparents.

Grandpa nodded permission as his ice cream melted down the side of his cone. Carson studied Levi, looking for a sign of panic or dread. He seemed to be comfortable standing next to the officer. After introductions, Carson understood why. Levi had an uncle that Carson had never met or known about, Tom—Officer Tom.

Levi's uncle shared with their grandparents, the news of Officer Browne being a fake.

Grandma put her hand over her mouth. "Oh my, we had an intruder in our house?"

"How was this discovered?" Grandpa asked.

Levi was beaming with pride while he explained. "The cop's uniform had his name stitched above the pocket, but the cops here wear gold name pins." He pointed to his uncle's shirt. "So I made a mental note of the officer's badge number. When we looked it up, it was invalid."

"Not to mention, there is not an Officer Browne working anywhere in this county," Tom said. "I've been trying to tell Levi not to associate with kids who get in trouble on the island. If you do, it's only a matter of time before trouble rubs off on you. I believe this has helped Levi understand my meaning."

"We are certainly glad to know Levi has learned a valuable lesson, and I hope Carson and Emma have, too," Grandpa said smiling. Then his smile faded. "What will be done about the man pretending to be a police officer? What was his motive?"

"I can't answer that yet. We need you to come to the station and file a report about the intruder's visit. Then we'll start investigating."

Whatever else was said by Levi's uncle faded into the background as the familiar sound of a Mustang grabbed Carson's attention. The cowboy was driving, and his arm was around a redhead. Carson quickly looked away when Kim flashed her pearly whites in his direction. Even though she had given him the bag back, he wasn't ready to return the cordial gesture.

Levi's voice brought Carson back to the conversation. "Is it okay if I come over tomorrow?"

Grandma gave Levi a hug as she said, "Of course you can."

Levi looked at Emma with a shy smile, and then put his hand up for Carson to give him a high five. Carson was pleasantly surprised to see his longtime friend being himself again.

"How did you remember the badge number?" Grandma asked Levi.

"Just lucky, I guess," Levi said, giving Emma and Carson a wink.

Emma's eyes twinkled. It was obvious that she was happy that the summer trio was back together again. That evening, just as the sun was setting, Carson and Emma stood on the beach. The horizon was painted with gold, and several shades of red, creating an ocean of pink waves. A few families were camping on the shore. Carson could almost taste the marshmallows being roasted over their campfires. Carson and Emma drew in the sand with their index fingers, playing tic-tac-toe.

After the third game with no winner, Emma said, "I wonder why a tied game is called a cat's game."

"It's the middle word spelled backward. Tic-*tac*-toe," said Carson.

"Oh, how did you know this little fun fact?" Emma asked.

"Levi," he said simply.

"I will never understand why he hides his intelligence—and his memory. That is such a cool ability." She drew a line through three X's.

"Speaking of cats, I saw Kim with the cowboy. They were in his Mustang," Carson said.

"The cowboy is Dean Jones, *remember*? They must know each other." Emma shrugged. "So what?"

"Kim is supposedly from out of town, *remember*? I am beginning to smell a rat."

CHAPTER TEN

Carson was awakened by his phone ringing full blast into his ear. He had ended the call with his dad last night and fallen asleep with the phone still on the pillow. Scared out of his sleep, he rolled off of his bed and hit the floor with a thud. When he picked up his phone, which had fallen with him, he saw it was Levi calling.

"This better be good," Carson groaned into the phone. "What's all the background noise?"

Levi sounded hyper. "I'm riding my skateboard. I've got something to show you and Emma."

"What is it?"

"Meet me on the pier, pronto!" Levi paused. "You may want to bring some gum." Then the call ended. This sounded like it would be another crazy day in paradise, but Carson was thrilled.

Carson and Emma waited an hour, but Levi never arrived. They tried calling and texting him several times but received no response.

"Did Levi sound scared when he called you this morning?" Emma asked.

"I thought he sounded excited," Carson paused. "But he was right about something."

"What?"

"I need some gum." Carson unwrapped three pieces and tossed them in his mouth. "I'm worried. Something bad must have happened," he said.

Emma tightened her ponytail. "Let's go the way Levi would have gone to get here. Show me the way."

"Maybe we should let Levi's uncle know he's missing."

"Let's not rush it," Emma said as she wiped grape spit from her forehead. "By the way—say it, don't spray it."

"Oops."

Carson and Emma didn't have far to go.

Levi was sitting on the gravel driveway of a cottage nearby. His skateboard was about twenty feet away from him, underneath an old mailbox. Levi sat with his knees drawn up to his chest, his arms encircling them, his head down and his face was buried in his knees.

Carson and Emma collapsed beside him. They gasped when he raised his head to look at them. His face had a mixture of dirt, tears, and blood smeared all over it. His right eye had begun to swell.

Levi hid his face back into his arms. "I didn't want you to see me like this." He sniffed rapidly a couple of times, like every kid does after a major meltdown.

Carson wondered if Levi would appreciate Emma sympathizing, so he shot her a look.

"Levi, what happened?" she said. "What do you need us to do?" Emma put her arm around his shoulders. "We're your best friends, *remember?*"

Was the word "*remember*" a sign for the trio? Carson wondered.

Levi allowed Emma to assist him standing up while Carson retrieved the skateboard.

"Don't take me to your grandparents. They'll get upset and worried, and maybe not let you or Emma out of the house this summer," Levi insisted. "I'll clean up in the ocean. The salt will clean my nose and eye better anyway, so I'll heal faster."

"You seriously need to be a doctor or something," Emma said.

Levi grinned slightly, accepting a compliment on his "smarts" for the first time.

Carson rolled his eyes when he heard the rumble of a Mustang pulling into the gravel driveway. Why was Dean Jones always around when something was happening?

"You kids need some help?" the cowboy asked, rolling down his window.

Carson saw red. He ignored the question, drawing the conclusion that this loser had something to do with his best friend getting beat up. "What's it to you? What are you doing here?" Carson snapped at him.

There was silence for a few seconds. Dean Jones gazed down the long driveway to the old cottage. Then he looked back at them and said, "I live here, Carson."

Carson felt his mouth drop open, though he tried to stop it. *This* was the cottage he talked about with Ms. Doris at the gas station. This whole time, the cowboy had been their neighbor.

Emma broke the uncomfortable silence. "Thank you, sir, but we can manage. Have a good day." She smiled sweeter than usual, apparently trying to make up for Carson's outburst.

With Levi limping in between, they finally made it down to the shore. All three of them waded waist-deep into the water.

The water felt refreshing to Carson's skin under his clothes. He realized it had been too long since he took advantage of having what Grandma called, "focus on the lighthouse" fun. She used to worry that Carson and Levi would end up going too far out, because they were too busy swimming. The rule was to look at the lighthouse every time they came up for air. Carson understood, since people often drowned in the ocean.

Emma's eyes were big as baseballs, even though she had put her glasses inside her shoes. "I have never been in the ocean. I've always been too scared," she admitted.

"Well, what do you think?" Levi asked, splashing his face one more time. He already looked like he was feeling better.

Emma smiled bigger than Carson had ever seen. "It feels exhilarating!" She dove into the next wave, free as a mermaid.

For the moment, they didn't think about ghosts, fires or fake cops. The next wave was all that mattered. Minutes turned into hours. Carson kept an eye on Emma since she was only now learning Grandma's rule. Finally, exhausted, they crash-landed on the shore.

The orange biplane did its daily flyby. The flames painted on the side seemed to bring the case back into their minds. All at once they sat up, facing each other.

"What happened on the way over, Levi?" Emma asked.

Levi glanced over at Carson. "Remember the older kid from the skate park? While I was on my way to meet you guys, he ran up and knocked me off of my skateboard and started whaling on me. While he was punching on me, he said he'd been asked to deliver a message. After he was done kicking my butt, he threw a balled-up piece of paper at me. He also took what I had in my back pocket."

Carson didn't know which he wanted to know first—what was taken or what was thrown. It didn't matter. Levi chose. He reached over to one of his shoes and pulled out the ball of paper.

Emma put on her glasses as Levi handed her the typed message. She read aloud.

To: The Summer Trio,

I know you have the diary. If you so much as lift a rock looking for the treasure, this beating Levi had and the fire will be nothing compared to what will be done to you. My recent actions and visit should suffice, in demonstrating that I will take whatever means necessary.

The treasure is rightfully mine.

"Officer Browne" lol

Emma practically spit fire. "This jerk actually wrote LOL." She handed the paper to Carson. "This must be a game to this freak," she added.

Carson shook his head, "What were you going to show us?"

"Luckily, it was something I read last night, so it's still here," Levi pointed to his head. "It was an article written three years ago with Kim's photo next to it."

"Kim? You had an article from three years ago?" Emma asked.

"Yeah, my mom keeps old newspapers. She does a lot of painting projects and shipping. The picture of Kim caught my attention when I was grabbing some paper for a package my mom asked me to get ready."

"All right, what did the article say about Kim?" Carson asked.

"It was apparent that she's a *ghost hunter*. She writes books about her encounters. The book she was writing at the time of the article was called *The Lovelorn Ghost of St. Simons.*"

"I knew there was something scary about that redhead," Carson bragged. "We need to get a copy of the book."

"It was never published," Levi said. "I checked last night."

"Well, then, we need to talk to Kim. Ask her some questions."

Carson crossed his arms. "I'm not going near her. She might curse us or something."

"Don't be ridiculous, she's a ghost hunter, not a witch," Emma said. "We need to find out where Minnie Mae Murphy is trying to lead us. Levi, finding a three-year-old article about a ghost hunter is *not* a coincidence."

⊱⊰

Emma started drawing in the sand. It looked like the list she mentioned on the lighthouse balcony yesterday.

Carson studied the message from the fake cop again. He noticed a smudge on the note. It was light yellow, almost white. He ran his thumb over it. It was smooth but hard, yet soft enough to make a dent with his fingernail.

"What is it?" Levi asked, seeing Carson fidget with the paper.

"Whoever typed this message dropped something on it. Not sure what, though."

Emma took the note. She put the smudge to her nose. "It smells familiar. Like…maybe…ice cream."

"There is no way its ice cream," Carson replied, as he took the note back to smell it. He raised his eyebrows in surprise. "It kind of smells like…birthday cake."

Levi snatched it and put it to his nose. "I don't smell anything."

"You got hit in the nose too hard or something," Carson said. "It definitely has a scent. The texture is what I don't get."

"Never mind the message for now," Emma impatiently swiped at the sticky sand on her clothes. "We have a ghost hunter to interrogate."

⊷⊶

CHAPTER ELEVEN

"So, here are our questions surrounding the case," Emma said, crunching into an apple and reading what she'd written in her notebook. "One, who is Officer Browne? Two, where has he put the treasure map? Three, is there a buried treasure? Four, what does Kim know about Minnie Mae Murphy? And five, does Dean Jones' have any involvement with Kim and the ghost?"

The house was empty, since Grandma was off doing errands and Grandpa was off at the lighthouse. After showering off the sand, the kids sat around the kitchen table to snack and strategize.

"Here's what we know about the culprit," Levi said as he tossed a muffin wrapper into the trash. "He has the treasure map from the diary. He is dangerous, and warns us to stay out of his way. He works with disguises and is obviously willing to ruin us, or possibly take other desperate measures to sidetrack us, in order to steal the treasure."

"He's bold enough to break into the house, but sloppy," Carson added. "He dropped a lighter in my room." Carson told Levi about the cigarette lighter.

"We need to investigate the entry Minnie Mae showed us in the shack," Emma said. Carson and Levi nodded in agreement.

"Mike knows about the ghost," Carson said. "His phone call started this whole thing. What if whoever he was talking to on the phone is the culprit?"

"We would need his phone records. The police can't get copies of phone records without a warrant, so that's out of the question for us," Levi said.

"What do we have so far then?" Emma asked.

"We have the diary and the key. We have the balled-up message," Levi said dryly. "We *did* have the lighter, the map page, and the article on Kim."

"So, if I were a ghost hunter, where would I be on a day like this?" Emma asked.

Carson looked out the window. Dark clouds had formed a blanket, covering the sky. "The two places we've seen her is around the lighthouse and with the cowboy." Carson stood up. "Let's go pay our neighbor a visit."

The cottage next door had been vacant every summer Carson had visited. His grandparents said the place had been undergoing restoration many years ago, but for unknown reasons, the work had never been completed. The cottage had remained empty until the day Dean Jones moved in.

The cottage definitely spoke of neglect. Its white paint was cracked and peeling. The windows were coated with sand and mildew. The wrap around porch had several boards broken or missing. A porch swing hung to the floor on one side, giving the house the appearance of a frown.

The property was the same size as the lighthouse property, about three acres wide. Palm trees had grown majestically between the ocean and the ramshackle cottage, and were the only decorative feature of the forsaken dwelling.

Carson imagined that long ago this cottage had been homey and inviting, but now it was harsh and bleak. It would make an impressive haunted house for Halloween. At that moment, a bolt of lightning flashed, as if playing along with Carson's imagination. He counted to three before hearing thunder.

No Mustang was in the driveway. "Well, it appears nobody is home," Carson said nervously. "Maybe we should come back later."

"No," Levi disagreed. "This is a perfect investigative opportunity." He walked up to the front door and turned the handle. The door opened easily.

To Carson's dismay, Emma nodded to Levi as if granting permission to trespass. As soon as they entered the cottage, Carson felt butterflies take flight inside his stomach. The air inside was stale. It smelled pungent and musky. Carson struggled to breathe, smothered by the fear of being caught. What if the cowboy came home while they were snooping? Carson was sure they would be arrested. Even grape gum wouldn't help Carson's dreadful state of anxiety, so he tried to focus on his friends instead.

"Don't turn on any lights," Levi warned. "Your eyes will adjust in a few minutes."

"What if we don't have a few minutes and we get caught?"

"Don't jinx us," Emma whispered. "We're investigating, so get your mind right."

Rain beat loudly on the old tin roof like a steady drum, intensifying the dramatic mood. Carson felt the urge to scream in hopes of making the rain stop, which made no sense, he realized. *Carson, snap into Agent Maverick mode*, he told himself.

The front room was furnished with a worn brown leather couch with a matching recliner chair. The room next to that contained a complicated setup of weird-looking stereo components and technical devices covered with knobs. The modern equipment looked out of place in the antique environment.

The wooden floor had a big round rug in the middle with running horses stitched into it. They probably wanted to gallop out of this dispiriting place.

"Hey, you guys, come into the kitchen," Levi called out over the pounding rain.

"Shush!" Carson whispered. "Not so loud."

"This is Kim's stuff. All these notes are related to the lighthouse. It looks like she's started working on her ghost book again."

Emma slid a beach bag from underneath the table. She pulled out makeup, sunscreen, hair clips, and a towel. "Kim must be staying here quite a bit."

Levi stopped looking through a kitchen drawer. "Remember what Dean Jones said to us in Teddy's barbershop? He warned us about ghosts from personal experience. Now it makes sense.

Carson was starting to feel calm, yet eager to learn more about the mysterious cowboy and ghost hunter. "Look for the treasure map. It must be here somewhere." He halted when he heard a sound.

>=<+ +>=<

The floor creaked in the other room, as though someone was standing on a squeaky board. That was followed by a sound like something being shuffled around.

Since all three kids were in the kitchen, Carson realized it had to be Dean Jones, Kim, or both. His heart dropped to his stomach. This felt a thousand times worse than the time he had been caught unwrapping a Christmas gift after bedtime. He saw that Levi and Emma were frozen in place, too. He wasn't the only one hearing the floor shift.

There was nowhere for them to go. Not until Levi jumped onto the counter like a cat, and pushed a window up in one movement. He motioned for Emma to go first. She bounded onto the counter and dove through the open window with impressive form. Carson felt inspired. He followed her example, but landed face-first on the sand. After spitting out a mouthful of sand, the air was knocked out of his chest when ninety pounds landed on him.

"Sorry!" Levi whispered, rolling off of him. The rain had slowed to a refreshing sprinkle, and the air outside felt cool and invigorating. Carson had never run so fast in all of his life. He was impressed by Emma keeping up, but she did, all the way to the angel oak. They fell to their knees on the wet grass.

Carson looked at Levi and Emma's white faces, and began laughing uncontrollably. The other two joined the contagious outburst. Carson rolled on the ground, holding his aching abdomen muscles.

"Do you think we were seen?" Emma asked between breaths.

"No way," Levi shook his head laughing. "We flew like the wind."

"They're going to know someone broke in," Carson said. "We left the kitchen window open. And we moved things out of place."

"So? They won't know it was us. Now we know where to start looking for the treasure map." Levi smiled with apparent satisfaction.

Carson shook the rain out of his hair like a dog. "This is getting too crazy," he said, lowering his voice. "I can't believe we broke into a house, and you're talking as if it will happen again."

"Not necessarily," Emma said, wiping her fogged glasses with her shirt. "We have a safer angle to work for now. I think we've been neglecting the most valuable evidence of all." She raised her eyebrows as if she expected the boys to fill in the blank.

"The diary," Carson said.

"Exactly," Emma said smiling. "We need to read the secrets of a ghost's diary."

CHAPTER TWELVE

The sun peaked behind a vanishing cloud, drying Carson's damp clothes and warming the air to extra humid, midday summer heat. Carson thought Emma and Levi looked like drowned rats, but he didn't say so since he probably did too. His stomach growled instead, sounding like a bear after months of hibernation.

Emma giggled, saying, "I agree. It's time for lunch."

They walked into the kitchen and were greeted with smiles. Their grandparents were already halfway finished eating Greek salads loaded with roast beef, pastrami, and feta cheese. If Carson had to eat a salad, this looked better than most.

"Yum, my favorite," Emma licked her lips.

"Why doesn't that surprise me?" Levi shook his head.

"If it was up to you, we'd be having Skittles wrapped in Laffy Taffy for lunch," Emma said, punching Levi lightly in the arm.

"Well," Grandma said laughing, "it looks like the summer trio is back to normal." She put a big salad bowl in front of each of them at the table.

Carson ate everything but the black olives. They always reminded him of the fat beetles that landed under lights at night.

"Carson and Levi, I want you to know that Teddy is in good health and home now. He says the new barbershop will be built soon, at the same place." Grandpa patted the boys on the head as he relayed the good news.

"I think it would be wonderful if you three went to visit him," Grandma chimed in. "No reason not to, since the policeman who said to stay away wasn't really a policeman."

"Have the real police been able to find out anything about him?" Emma asked.

"No, the only thing they've said is that nobody else has called the station about an Officer Browne," Grandma replied with a shrug. "He seems to have vanished."

"Doesn't make any sense why someone would do that," Grandpa added, shaking his head. "I checked the house and nothing seems to be missing."

Carson looked at Emma and Levi, wondering if they should tell them about the diary. Emma shot a warning look, so he decided against it.

They were on their own. Carson was getting more paranoid each day that something bad might happen. What if Officer Browne ended up being a killer or kidnapper? The message he wrote dripped with insanity.

If the diary didn't uncover enough clues, they would end up breaking into the cowboy's cottage again to look for evidence. An hour later Carson, Levi, and Emma arrived at the hideout shack on the beach.

⊨⊱ ⊰⊨

"You guys, don't laugh," Emma said with a serious face, "but I've been thinking about what we've read in the diary from a girl's perspective."

"Well, that makes sense. It was written by a girl. You might know how to take it better than we would," Levi said with a shrug.

Emma looked relieved. "After all Minnie Mae went through with pirates and the treasure, she wrote more passionately about Joseph. This is a love story, and I think the answers might be found in the entries about him."

Levi looked up as if he saw information files falling out of the walls. "Let me think. Minnie Mae began working for the lighthouse in 1893. In 1898, a year before Joseph Martin died, she wrote that he asked her to marry him, but she declined. Joseph died six years after they met, in 1899. She wrote that his blood was on her hands, which I believe means she felt partially responsible somehow. She wrote that she should have kept things to herself instead of sharing them with Joseph," Levi paused. "You may be right, Emma. Everything we know so far revolves around their relationship."

"In the last entry," Emma said, pointing to the diary, "her writing sounds like she was planning to leave, so she decided to draw the treasure map. Why would she run away?"

"Maybe she was afraid something would happen to her," Carson stated.

"Either way, Minnie Mae concludes that destiny will suffice. Over a hundred years later, destiny is fulfilled—through us!" Emma exclaimed.

"Yeah, except some lunatic stole the treasure map," Levi grunted.

"I wonder what happened in her life after she finished the diary?" It was Emma's turn to gaze at the wall, as if seeing a vision. "She sounds amazing; I would have loved to know her. Can you imagine all the stories she could tell?"

Carson took the diary and flipped through it, looking for nothing in particular but following a hunch. He stopped when he saw a drawing. "I wonder why this drawing is in the diary." Carson held it out so they could all study it.

It was a simple diagram of a tree, dated five months after Joseph died. One of the branches was labeled with an M, the one beside with a J, and the branch in the middle—drawn higher than the other two—wasn't labeled. Below each labeled branch was another set of branches.

Emma leaned closer to get a better look as she pushed her glasses up. "This reminds me of a family tree. My teacher brought hers to class last year, an extensive one going back hundreds of years. We had to make one for our family, but only for two generations."

"All right, it's obvious…"

Carson cut Levi off. "Let me sound smart for once. The M is for Minnie Mae Murphy and the J is for Joseph Martin."

"Okay, smarty, so who is the middle branch without a label?"

The boys looked at the family tree expert.

Emma put her hand over her mouth. "Minnie Mae had a baby."

A shiver went up Carson's spine. He suddenly felt the urge to cry. Then he realized it was because he heard a low and steady sob. It was a heart-wrenching sound, similar to when his mom had cried at his baby sister's funeral. He squeezed his eyes shut, trying to push the feelings back down inside. The lost and lonely feeling Carson had each time the ghost haunted them closed in on him so violently he thought his chest would break in two. Carson looked at Emma to see if she was crying but there were no tears. She sat on the floor, shivering, with crossed arms, looking from Levi to him with a sorrow-filled expression.

Levi covered his ears with his hands. The mournful weeping seemed to come from every corner of the room, and then it seemed to stop directly in front of them.

"Look," Levi said, pointing to the floor in the middle of them. An invisible finger wrote in the dirt on the floor, one word.

Carson read it aloud with a shaking voice, "BETRAYED."

Then the forgotten picture flew out of the bag and landed on top of the open diary. The picture of the light-house from Carson's room didn't land facing up. It landed with the back staring up at them. The ghost left and the warmth of the room returned. The silence was the most beautiful sound to Carson's ears.

Emma snatched the picture up to look at what was written in the upper right corner. She spoke the letters: "MMM."

"Am I missing something?" Levi asked.

"Remember the lighter Carson told you about? It had this same thing engraved on it," Emma said.

"I knew the word *remember* would be significant some-how, and now it makes sense," Carson said.

"What, genius?" Levi smirked.

"We have all the evidence to solve this case. We just have to put our heads together and *remember* the clues to piece it together."

In the next instant they all screamed as the door to the shack flew open and a flashlight shone into the dark room.

CHAPTER THIRTEEN

The first image Carson saw once the light wasn't blinding him was snakeskin cowboy boots. Behind those were pink flip-flops covered in rhinestones. That's all it took for Carson's throat to feel as if a bullfrog had moved in. He knew if he tried to talk, it would sound like a croak.

Kim was the first to speak. "So, what do we have here?"

Levi seemed angry about his hiding spot being exposed. "How did you find us?"

"Don't be ridiculous," Kim spouted. "I'm aware of any building that's one hundred years or older on the island. You three snooping kids know I'm a ghost hunter, so this shouldn't be a surprise." Kim flipped her hair behind her shoulders.

Dean Jones took one step forward, so the kids took two steps back. *Did he always have a knife in his belt or is it there just for the day, and intended for us?* Carson wondered.

The cowboy reached for something on his belt. Immediately courage he never knew existed erupted in Carson like a volcano. He stepped in front of his cousin and friend, stretching his arms out wide in front of them. "I'm warning you. Come any closer and I'll make you regret ever being born." Carson could only guess at what it meant, but he'd heard it in a cowboy and Indian show once.

"Take it easy, kid. I just want to show you something," Dean said, as he pulled out his cell phone.

Carson was confused, and hoped there wasn't a new cell phone that could be used as a firearm. Ironically, what Dean showed them on his phone *was* a weapon that could be used against them, though not a firearm. It was a video that had obviously been recorded a few hours ago. It contained footage of Carson, Levi, and Emma entering and sneaking around the cowboy's cottage.

Carson remembered seeing the stereo and technical equipment in the cottage, thinking it all looked out of place. It had been recording everything. Feeling lightheaded, Carson plopped down on the floor, as though the air had been kicked out of him. Emma and Levi sat down next to him. It was as if they gave up all at once.

"Since the video I've shown you seems to have sunk in," Dean said with a chuckle, "I'll explain."

"Why should you get all the fun?" Kim snapped. "Let me take it from here."

"Zip it, little sister," Dean said. "I already told you, I'm doing the talking. You get too...riled up."

Emma pushed her glasses up. "Did you just say she was your sister?"

Kim put her hands on her hips. "Are you telling me, you nosy brats don't know that Dean and I are brother and sister? I've given these amateurs too much credit, Dean."

Dean shot Kim a *shut your mouth* look.

"Listen, kids," Dean said calmly. "I have no intention of reporting this intriguing movie..."

Kim interrupted, "...unless you don't cooperate."

Another look shot between the two siblings.

Dean continued, "The equipment you saw in the cottage is my sister's. I bought the place because we *knew* it was haunted. All the equipment you saw is used for ghost hunting. Now, don't think I'm crazy for choosing to live in a haunted house. The only reason I agreed to it was because we're familiar with this particular ghost. Kim has sort of made..." Dean paused, "Minnie Mae Murphy an obsession. The cottage was Minnie Mae's home when she worked for the lighthouse keeper in the 1800s."

Carson felt his eyes grow bigger than beach balls. "It wasn't you who came home when we were in the cottage, was it?"

Dean and Kim started laughing, which gave Carson his answer.

Emma looked at Kim with new admiration and said, "Isn't Minnie Mae cool? I would love to hear all you have learned about her."

The statement seemed to make an instant connection between the two.

"I would enjoy trading information," Kim said with the first genuine smile Carson had seen.

Levi spoke up. "No, Emma. We aren't trading anything with this happy little family."

Kim resumed her glare and pointed at Levi. "Oh, yes, you will, or I will march straight to the police station. In fact, I'll make sure to ask for your uncle."

"Let's try to be cordial with one another," Dean stated. "We all want the same thing here—to solve the mystery surrounding Minnie Mae."

Carson was sure he saw flames fly out of Levi's eyes.

"First, tell us where you hid the treasure map," Levi spat. The shack they were in was silent for the amount of time it takes between birthdays—forever.

Kim spoke her next words slowly and carefully. "Minnie Mae Murphy shared her diary with you three kids. Surely you know where the map is. Even after seeing it on the pier, I could hardly believe she chose you three." A look of bewilderment was plastered on Kim's face.

Carson felt consumed by curiosity. He asked, "What do you mean by…the ghost *shared* it with us?"

"You three are disappointing me with your lack of knowledge, so far," Kim said, shaking her head. She sat down on the floor with them and continued. "Legend says that Minnie Mae Murphy wrote a diary, but when she ran away with her baby, she took it with her. Nobody has ever seen it. She haunts the lighthouse every summer looking for someone to give the diary to. It's the only thing of hers still in existence today that I *don't* have. And as far as I know, it's also the only record that ever contained the map to the buried treasure. I only gave the diary back to you that day on the porch because I have a….healthy respect for the spirit world."

Carson, Emma, and Levi looked at one another, not sure what to say. Carson knew they didn't have a choice but to tell Kim and Dean everything. Carson was still not totally convinced that they could be trusted, but it didn't matter at this point. He didn't want to have a criminal record. The risk of telling them about the diary was their only option.

Emma asked Kim, "Are you both so interested in Minnie Mae because she is your great-great-grandmother?"

"No, we're not related. But I've been intrigued with her since I was your age, Emma. Probably for the same reasons you think Minnie Mae is cool," said Kim. "But I've known about her for a long time. Our great-great-grandmother was friends with Minnie Mae. They worked together."

"We may have read about her," Carson said. "In one of the diary entries, Minnie Mae asked a trusted friend to sneak around the docks to find out if pirates were asking about her."

Carson's mom had always told him that the truth was like a bell. When you hear it, it rings true. He knew what she meant now. Kim was telling the truth and Dean Jones did not steal the map from his room. He was not the fake cop. He was not the one who had Levi beaten up. They were both innocent.

As Carson began telling them about the previous days, his thinking became clear. When he spoke of the odd events, the ghost and the diary, clues of the case fell into place. He *remembered* details that were hidden before.

"Carson, I can practically see light bulbs dancing above your head," Emma said laughing, "What part of this mystery have you solved?"

Carson was enjoying the moment, and he wanted them to feel the same satisfaction. So, he didn't just blurt out the answer. "The smudge on the balled-up message was candle wax. It smelled like cake or ice cream because it was *vanilla scented*," Carson said.

Levi added, "Right! And the wax came from your grandmother's candles in the museum. So-called Officer Browne...that's Mike! And he had access to costumes because he builds sets for the theater."

Emma was shaking her head, "Of course. Mike, the lighthouse keeper, works for our grandparents, so he waited until they were too busy to notice him entering the house, and stole the map from Carson's room."

"Levi, when you were looking through the employee files that night in the museum, did you notice what the lighthouse keeper's full name is?"

"His name is Michael Matthew Murphy. MMM. His initials match the engraved lighter and back of the light-house picture."

Carson spoke what they all knew. "Mike is the perpetrator."

Emma looked like she could cry, saying, "And Mike must be the great-great-grandson of Minnie Mae Murphy."

"No wonder Minnie Mae feels betrayed," Carson said as he wiped a bead of sweat from his forehead. The door to the shack slowly creaked open, and framed in the door-way, backlit by the sun, was the figure of a man. He was clapping slowly as if he had just watched the ending to a theatrical play.

CHAPTER FOURTEEN

When Michael Murphy stepped through the doorway, Carson immediately noticed the gun shoved into the side of his belt. Carson was skeptical about whether the gun was real, or part of the Officer Browne costume.

"Shouldn't you be attending to your lighthouse duties, Mike?" Levi asked sarcastically. "Or did you come to beat me up yourself this time?"

The confidence Carson heard in Levi's voice was contagious. Carson continued the game of mockery. "Are you here to arrest us, *Officer Browne*, or did you return the plastic badge to the theater already?"

Mike took out a cigarette from his shirt pocket and casually lit it with the engraved lighter. He blew out smoke as he said, "I knew after Carson gave me back my lighter that it wouldn't take long for the summer trio to blow my cover."

Emma stood up and put her hands on her hips. "How could you betray your own grandmother?"

"The way I see it," Mike snapped, "Minnie Mae Murphy betrayed me! I've been working as a lighthouse keeper to win her affections. She should have given the diary to me. Then you three sneak into the lighthouse one night, and the ghost gives you what's rightfully mine. I'm the only living Murphy. That treasure is my inheritance."

Kim stood up next and asked, "I'm confused, Mike. If you stole the treasure map, what are you doing here?"

"Of course I took the treasure map, but the directions are written with symbols. Turns out, I need the diary to decipher what the symbols mean," Mike snorted. "She was smarter than I thought."

Kim's temper flew out like a cat out of water. "Minnie Mae was smart. She watched you live long enough to see your true colors somewhere along the way. These kids and I know it was a mournful decision for Minnie, not to give the diary to her own flesh and blood. But she was right. Why would she give the diary to a good-for-nothing—" Kim stopped midsentence when Mike pulled a gun on her.

Mike pointed the gun back and forth between Kim and Dean saying, "This matter has nothing to do with either of you, but I can't let you leave just yet." He paused and looked around the room. "Carson, take that rope from over there in the corner and tie them up. Do a good job if you want to make it to another summer."

Mike must have seen the doubt in Carson's eyes. He opened the clip of the gun and revealed a loaded chamber of bullets. After snapping it back in place, he added, "Tie them up now."

With shaking knees, Carson knelt down to pick the rope up from the floor. He felt like a coward obeying the jerk with a loaded gun. As Carson walked behind Emma, he saw the diary on the floor behind her feet. Mike would no doubt demand the diary next. Carson imagined he would leave town with it to let things cool off, and come back for the treasure later. He did not want to let that happen. Minnie Mae had entrusted them with the diary, and now they were letting her down.

Mike sounded irritated when he spoke. "I'm not going to say it again. Tie their hands to each other behind their backs. Over in the corner, away from the window."

Carson stalled, knowing he was about to tie up the best hope of getting the gun away from Mike. Dean was the biggest guy there.

Mike grabbed Emma by the arm and pointed the gun at her. Levi screamed, "If you hurt her, I swear, I'll—"

"You'll what, you little loser?" Mike cackled. "Shut up, Levi. Go stand with your nose in the corner." He nodded his head to the corner behind the stove.

"Now, or I'll put a bullet in your girlfriend's pretty face," Mike said, between clenched teeth. Levi had his nose in the corner before Mike finished his threat.

While Carson tied the rope around Dean's hands, he saw the knife again, hanging from Dean's belt. The darkness of the room was in their favor. With his back toward Mike, Carson slipped the knife out of its holster and put it in Dean's hand before tying Kim's hand over it. Carson slowly turned around to face Mike, who still had the gun pointed at Emma.

Emma stared at Carson with dread. Tears slid down her cheek. Was she crying out of fear or regret? Either way, it broke his heart, and he wanted to hurt Mike more than ever.

Suddenly, a loud and heavy thud hit the floor behind Carson. Dean had dropped the knife. Sour stomach acid filled Carson's mouth.

Levi swung around to see what the noise had been. Their eyes locked and Carson knew it was time to act. Emma must have seen the unspoken plan between Carson and Levi because she yelled, "Now!"

Carson dove for the knife as Levi lunged for Mike's feet. Emma knocked the gun out of Mike's hand as he struggled to keep his balance. The gun slid toward Carson, who was frantically cutting through the rope. *Should he keep cutting the rope to free Dean or grab the gun?* Carson stared at the weapon with terror. He had never held a gun, and didn't want this to be a first. What if he accidently killed Mike? The thought compelled Carson to kick the gun farther away from Mike. Cutting the rope was the safer option.

He stopped when he heard the smack of Mike's hand hitting flesh. Emma fell to the floor with an ear-piercing scream. Then Mike pushed Levi against the wall. A board cracked from the hard impact of Levi's head. He slid to the floor, looking dazed.

Mike pounced on the gun like a lion to take possession of it. Carson did the only thing he could think of to make Mike drop the weapon—he threw the knife in his hand at the lower part of Mike's body. It worked. Mike dropped the gun when the blade pierced his right thigh.

"No!" Mike yelled in obvious disbelief. He sunk to the floor, holding his bleeding wound.

Reality seemed to move in slow motion for Carson from that moment on. All the sound in the world muted. With just the sound of his heart pounding, Carson took one step at a time toward the gun. Breathing as if he were swimming against a current, Carson bent down and picked up the loaded gun. It felt heavy in his hand, and the black metal was cool against his hot skin. Carson cocked the gun like he had seen in movies. Then he pointed it at Mike. Carson felt horribly powerful, but in control.

Carson heard himself talking, as if in a dream. "Emma, are you okay?"

Emma answered with relief, "I'm fine."

"Levi?" Levi nodded.

"Don't shoot, please!" Mike squealed, still holding his bleeding thigh. "You can have the map and the diary. I promise I'll go far away and never come back again." He pulled the map from his shirt pocket and threw it toward Carson.

Emma picked it up off the floor and put it in the bag with the diary.

Levi walked over and untied Dean and Kim.

"The only place you'll be going is jail," Dean stated, as he walked over to Carson and lightly patted him on the back. "It's alright son, you did good. Now, give me the gun. I'll take it from here."

Carson blinked hard as the words registered. Still keeping the gun pointed at Mike, he slowly handed it to Dean, his favorite cowboy of all times.

Levi pulled his cell phone from his back pocket and for once, made a real 9-1-1 call. "There has been an attempted burglary. We need the police and an emergency vehicle." Levi shook his head. "There isn't an address. Listen to my directions carefully." After Levi ended the call, he shook his head, saying, "I'm going to need a new secret hideout."

CHAPTER FIFTEEN

The grandparents were mortified to find out the danger the kids had experienced. To know that a criminal had been working for them was disturbing as well. It seemed like a bad dream when Carson thought about the moment he had willingly hurt another human by throwing a knife. When the police said the incident was self-defense, Carson felt so relieved he could have jumped high enough to kiss the moon. But most of all, he was proud of the summer trio's teamwork.

After the police handcuffed Mike, they called him a "crazy case." His story about a ghost's diary containing a secret treasure map seemed ridiculous to them. It would be the joke of the week at the police station, Carson figured.

Levi came up with a great addition to their side of the story, saying that his mom had assigned him a history project, so they came up with the idea of creating a fictional diary. He told the police that Carson and Emma had been helping him to get the boring assignment over with faster. He gave the balled-up message from "Officer Browne" to the police as well.

Kim told the police that she and Dean had been walking on the beach when they heard a scream from inside the shack. Dean said they had rushed to help, but found that the kids had everything under control. They agreed with the police regarding Mike acting and talking irrationally.

Then Mike was taken away in the emergency vehicle, accompanied by a police car. The theme song from *Cops* played in Carson's head. He could hardly believe where this investigation had taken them.

Dean told the kids that they would be heading to Maine for his sister's next haunted house case.

"What about Minnie Mae?" asked Emma.

To their surprise, Kim told them that Minnie Mae Murphy was "their" ghost; she had chosen the kids, and Kim respected Minnie's choice. The kids agreed to keep their new friends posted on any future occurrences or findings.

Three days later Carson, Emma, and Levi met on the pier with the bag containing the diary and the treasure map.

The warm beach air felt like a cozy blanket to Carson. He breathed in through his nose for as long as he could. He had grown to love the salty smell with hints of fishiness. A piece of grape gum would go perfectly with the scent, so Carson popped a piece in his mouth.

Emma smiled saying, "We should call you the grape goblin. You can wear a purple cape and purple tights." She had been teasing her cousin about being a superhero for the last few days because of his heroic actions in the shack.

Carson would never admit it, but he enjoyed the notion. "Zip it," he playfully said.

Levi put his hands upside down against his face, forming a mask. He crossed his eyes and stuck his tongue out to the side. "Never fear, grape goblin is here."

"How original, Levi. Now if you're done, let's get down to business," Carson said, rolling his eyes.

Emma took the folded map from the bag. With her hand she ironed it flat unto the pier.

Carson shook his head to erase the image of Mike throwing the folded map toward him. He could feel his finger on the trigger even now.

Emma put her hand on Carson's. "Did you hear what Levi said?"

"No, sorry…" Carson saw understanding in both their eyes.

"I said Mike was wrong. He didn't need the diary to decipher these symbols."

"Are you serious?"

"Yeah, he was looking at the map through eyes of today. This map was drawn over a hundred years ago, so it's not going to look accurate to us. Plus, Minnie Mae didn't draw the entire island. She used symbols for landmarks, but she only drew the part of the island where the lighthouse was," Levi said, pointing to the obvious marking.

"So," Emma interjected. "We need to imagine we were at the scene at the time the treasure was buried."

Carson added, "Analyze the map in past tense and it will make sense."

"That's easy," Levi said smiling. "I learned about St. Simon's history in school." He looked at the map. "It all makes perfect sense to me."

Emma hugged Levi out of what seemed like a gut reaction. Carson swallowed a giggle when Levi turned red as a strawberry. Emma looked down at the diary and asked what must have been the first thing that popped in her head. "Why do pirates bury treasures, anyway? What's the point in having wealth if you're not going to spend it?"

"I know why," Carson replied. "Most of the time pirates buried the treasure during an escape, planning to go back at a later time. In some instances, they were captured and hung, so the treasure stayed unknown and buried. They also buried treasures to have wealth in places they visited often. It's not like pirates could just deposit their stash in a bank."

Levi added, "Plus, the valuables were stolen."

Emma nodded. "I understand why they had treasure maps, then. Otherwise, pirates would forget where they put all their treasures after long voyages, especially if they had several treasures to keep up with."

"What if a pirate already took the treasure we are seeking?" Carson asked.

"No way," Levi answered. "Minnie Mae wrote in her first diary entry that she moved and reburied the treasure twice after escaping."

"One day a long time ago, Captain Robert Riley had a bad day when he found an empty hole instead of his buried treasure," Emma said laughing.

"Yeah, he probably threw a big ole pirate's tantrum." Carson stood up, throwing his hands around while turning in circles.

"That just looks like you being you," Levi said with a smirk.

"If we're going to be treasure seekers in this decade, we need to stay focused." Emma pushed her glasses up as she studied the map.

It was interesting how Levi obeyed Emma as if he were a puppy dog. What had gotten into his tough skater friend? Carson wondered if Levi would continue hanging out with the tough skater kids after this summer. He was glad that Levi hadn't changed that much after all and that their friendship was stronger than ever.

Levi leaned in to get a closer look. "Obviously X marks the spot of the treasure. The site is next to the cross symbol, which happens to be where the second-oldest church still stands."

Carson put his hand over his mouth as he said, "Holy moly, the treasure is buried in the graveyard."

"Bingo."

CHAPTER SIXTEEN

At midnight Carson, Levi, and Emma met at what had become like a home base-the angel oak. They had agreed to dress in dark colors. It reminded Carson of the night they snuck into the museum. So much had happened since then. He felt sure his maturity level had grown higher than that of some grown men.

"I really wish we didn't have to do this at night," Emma complained.

"We can't dig up a buried treasure in the middle of the day," Carson said, "especially in a graveyard." He tried not to sound like the jitters had set in. Maybe he wasn't so manly after all.

They had brought trowels and a shovel for the mission. Levi carried an object that resembled a weed eater.

"A metal detector is a standard tool for treasure seekers. It's my Uncle Tom's."

"You stole from a cop?" asked Carson.

"No, I just borrowed it from his garage. I'll be returning it tonight, so he won't have a chance to miss it. We need a metal detector."

"Won't there be lots of metal in a grave yard? Like jewelry on....the buried?" Carson asked.

"Hey, you're getting smarter lately, but this will only detect shallow objects. I doubt Minnie Mae buried it real deep." He added. "At least, let's hope not."

"Can we please not argue? It's not helping my nerves," Emma pleaded.

Carson pulled out a pack of grape gum. "Anybody want some?"

To his surprise, Emma yanked a piece out and shoved it in her mouth. Between chews she whispered. "I have to get into detective mode." After she tightened her ponytail, a focused look replaced the worried one.

Carson wished it were that easy for him to focus. After popping three pieces of gum into his mouth, he said, "Let's go before...someone...before we change our minds."

"All right," Levi whispered. "Emma, do you have the diary and the map in case we need them?"

Emma looked insulted. "Are the stars shining?"

Carson tried not to look obvious as he looked up. Indeed, the stars twinkled like diamonds against a bluish-black sky. A single wispy cloud stretched in front of a full moon like a scarf. He wished he had one since the night air was cooler than expected. The ocean breeze made goose bumps on his arms so he picked up the pace to get further inland.

Emma asked, "Remember when we went through the graveyard and the branch fell and a spooky black cat showed up?"

Levi asked laughing, "Do cats' meow?"

Emma ignored the humor. "What if that day in the graveyard, Minnie Mae was trying to get our attention? Maybe we were walking right over the treasure!"

Carson was impressed. "Good point." Then he thought further about what Emma said.

Minnie Mae was cool, but he wasn't too keen on the idea of seeing a ghost in a graveyard at night. There wasn't any reason for her to show up, was there?

"Why would Minnie Mae bury the treasure in a grave-yard?" Carson asked.

"I think it was a great idea," Levi answered. "Even with a map showing the location, I bet most people would think it was a hoax."

The kids stayed quiet with their own thoughts until they reached the first grave. Levi broke the eerie silence. "Minnie Mae wrote that she moved the treasure to its final resting place the same day Joseph was buried."

"Well then... he must be buried here," Emma said hesitantly.

"Over there in the back," Carson pointed. "Those tombstones look really old."

They walked in a line with Levi leading, Emma in the middle, and Carson behind her. Nobody used a flashlight since the moon shone brightly. An owl suddenly hooted as if to ask who was there. Carson felt as though they were intruding on the laid-to-rest corpses. He tried to keep the images of what they might look like now out of his mind, but was failing miserably.

Emma turned her flashlight on and pointed it at the graves. Carson did the same. Black mildew had grown in the words carved into the stones, but they could read most of them. As Carson read random names and dates on headstones, he became curious about the deceased, about their families and their history. What had they done for fun? What kind of lives had they led? Suddenly, the metal detector beeped. Levi swung it above the ground like he was sweeping the grass. It made a static noise like their grandparents' old radio.

Emma dropped to her knees as she pointed her flashlight on a cross-shaped tombstone. Her mouth moved but no words came out. Carson ran over to her, almost tripping on the way. The name in the flashlight beam practically jumped out like a three-dimensional image.

"Minnie Mae Murphy is buried here," Carson squeaked.

On their knees, the trio stared in silence for several minutes, paying their respects. "She was born February 7,

1866, and died April 25, 1924," Levi read. "So, she died at the age of fifty-eight. Twenty-five years after Joseph died."

Seeing the grave after the experiences with her ghost and her diary gave Carson a whirlwind of emotions. It was as if he was visiting a friend's grave. He realized that Emma felt similar when she swiped a tear from her cheek.

Levi was searching again, apparently still in detective mode. "Quick, bring a flashlight!"

Carson and Emma jumped up and ran three rows back to Levi, who was standing at the foot of a grave. Carson pointed his flashlight at the tombstone. "Joseph Martin… March 3, 1854–August 7, 1899." The buzzing sounded more like an alarm in the quiet darkness.

"Shut that off, before somebody hears!" Emma said to Levi.

Silence followed. On their knees again, the three studied something on the ground. It seemed to gleam in spots, like a star in the moonlight. At first, only a tiny part was exposed. Levi took one of the trowels and scraped some of the dirt away, exposing a medallion the size of a silver dollar. On the front were two bones crisscrossed under a skull—the pirate symbol.

Levi pried up the medallion. "That's the coolest thing I have ever seen."

"It's starting to look like Minnie Mae buried the treasure right here, at Joseph's feet," Carson said.

"Not *with* his feet, right?" Emma asked. "Please tell me we aren't going to be digging Joseph Martin up."

Levi grabbed the shovel and started digging. "There's only one way to find out."

CHAPTER SEVENTEEN

Carson held the pirate medallion while Levi dug. The metal was surprisingly shiny and smooth. It was heavy for its size. Emma held her flashlight over the deepening hole in the ground. They were about to take turns digging when the shovel hit something at about three feet down. Levi bounced the shovel up and down. Several thuds confirmed there was an object underneath.

Jitters returned to Carson's stomach. He handed the medallion to Emma and got on his knees to start scraping dirt away with a trowel. Levi jumped on the shovel to loosen more of the dirt around the object.

What would be inside? Gold? Jewels? What if it ended up being nothing? That wasn't possible after all their efforts…was it?

"Wow," Emma said with a nervous laugh. "I can see something. It's a chest!" She tossed the flashlight down and starting digging beside Carson. Levi threw the shovel down and did likewise. The summer trio lifted the chest out of the ground together, setting it on the ground beside the pile of dirt.

Carson glanced around to make sure nobody was around. He picked up a flashlight to get a better look at the treasure chest.

A bronze looking trim outlined the black box. The shoebox sized chest was covered with an arched lid, like a treasure chest from the movies. It was in good shape for its age.

Emma ran her finger over the keyhole on the front of the chest. As if by instinct, she pulled out the diary. She took the key out of the diary lock and guided the key into the keyhole on the chest. It fit. They all gasped when Emma turned the key. The clicking noise was the sweetest sound to Carson's ears. He held his breath as Emma slowly lifted the lid.

A burgundy bag with a drawstring sat on top. Carson picked it up. It felt velvety soft.

"Open it!" Emma exclaimed.

Carson peered inside. "It's filled with coins." He took one out to get a closer look. "This looks like gold. There must be hundreds of them," Carson said.

Levi pulled out another smaller black box. "There's something else in there."

A woman's voice answered out of thin air. "Indeed there is."

Carson gasped when he looked up. Minnie Mae stood in front of them. Her form was visible, yet translucent. Carson wondered if her complexion had been as ghostly white when she was alive. Her eyes and hair were black as coal. She wore a long pale blue dress and brown boots that laced up the front. She looked as though she had stepped out of a history book. The air turned frigid, but the lost and lonely feeling no longer enveloped them in her presence. A feeling of peace and closure had replaced it.

"You are as beautiful as I imagined," Emma said. She was awestruck, as though a Hollywood star appeared instead of a ghost.

Minnie Mae smiled slightly and dipped her head politely with a small curtsey.

Levi surprised them by asking Minnie Mae's permission to open the smaller box. She nodded.

"There are three watches in here, but they look different from anything I've seen," Levi said as he studied them.

"Yes," Minnie Mae answered. "They *are* different from other watches. And there is one for each of you," she added.

Levi handed Carson and Emma each a watch.

Carson examined the gold watch in his hand. Its large round face held three small clocks. There were three tiny dials were on the outer and inner sides of the watch. The wristband had a gauge on it, which Carson assumed adjusted it to the owner's size. The decorative detailing in the gold was amazing.

"The watches are impressive," Carson stated, "but why do I have a feeling there is more to this story?"

The temperature dropped as Minnie Mae took three steps toward them. She bent toward the ground where they were sitting. Nobody moved back from her. Nobody was scared; they were only curious.

Minnie Mae reached her lucid arm forward as if she had an important announcement to make. "I have chosen the three of you to be an important team. You each have unique talents and gifts. Together, you will accomplish amazing things. Most importantly, you have pure hearts. I now declare the summer trio to be watch guardians."

Carson was anxious to know what she meant. "These watches don't just tell time, do they?"

Minnie Mae whispered words that rang in Carson's ears like a fire alarm.

"Indeed, these watches do not just *tell* time." She paused, then said solemnly, "They *travel* time."

"I'm sorry," Levi said. "I thought you said these watches can travel in time."

"You heard me correctly," Minnie Mae said with a nod. "So, it's imperative that no one ever sees them or, worse, takes them from you." When no one said anything, she continued. "The three watches will not work unless they are together. In order for you to time travel, each of the three watches must be set for the same place, date, and time."

Emma asked, "And the three small clocks on the face are used to set them? They indicate the place, date, and time to visit?"

Minnie Mae nodded with a proud smile as she looked at each of them. Then she whispered, "Travel well and accomplish much." She faded into the darkness.

Levi shook his head. "Wait! I have so many questions," he yelled. "Where did these watches come from?"

But it was too late. Minnie Mae was gone. "If we weren't just talking to a dead person, I would never have believed this." Levi shook his head. "Minnie Mae called us watch guardians! This is amazing!"

Carson looked at Emma, who had a wild look in her eyes.

"Let's test the time travel watches now!" She said, jumping up and down.

Carson wouldn't be able to sleep anyway, so he looked at his two best friends with a mischievous grin and said, "Why not? I was born to travel in time."

ABOUT THE AUTHOR

Dawn Marie Clifton was raised up in the Lord by her parents, Donald and Carolyn Taylor. She had the opportunity to travel the world while growing up and moved to Columbia, South Carolina, after graduating. Following a successful career in communications management, she went on to fulfill her dream of writing. Dawn graduated from the Institute of Children's Literature and has become a passionate author and novelist. She currently lives with her husband and family in Irmo, South Carolina.

Made in the USA
Monee, IL
14 September 2020